There was no way to preface this, so he met it head-on. "Kiera, it's not safe for you here."

She frowned, her eyes narrowing. "I don't like where this is going." She looked him in the eye as she stroked Lucy and the cat purred. "This is our home. I..."

"After what happened, Kiera, we can't take the chance that it might happen again."

"What do you mean?" she asked. "You and the other marshals are protecting me until the trial. I'm safe."

"You weren't safe yesterday afternoon."

"But I'm safe now," she insisted. "You make me safe."

He met her eyes, saw apprehension and something else—fear. He took her hands in both of his and pulled her close. His lips brushed Kiera's and then he was pulling her against him. He kissed her deeper.

When he let her go, she looked at him, befuddled.

WANTED BY
THE MARSHAL

—————

RYSHIA KENNIE

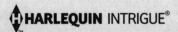

This book is dedicated to you, the reader. Enjoy!

ISBN-13: 978-1-335-60462-0

Wanted by the Marshal

Copyright © 2019 by Patricia Detta

Recycling programs
for this product may
not exist in your area.

This edition published by arrangement with Harlequin Books S.A.

For questions and comments about the quality of this book,
please contact us at CustomerService@Harlequin.com.

® and TM are trademarks of Harlequin Enterprises Limited or its
corporate affiliates. Trademarks indicated with ® are registered in the
United States Patent and Trademark Office, the Canadian Intellectual
Property Office and in other countries.

HARLEQUIN®
™ www.Harlequin.com

Printed in U.S.A.

Ryshia Kennie has received a writing award from the City of Regina, Saskatchewan, and was also a semifinalist for the Kindle Book Awards. She finds that there's never a lack of places to set an edge-of-the-seat suspense, as prairie winters find her dreaming of warmer places for heart-stopping stories. They are places where deadly villains threaten intrepid heroes and heroines who battle for their right to live, or even to love. For more, visit ryshiakennie.com.

Visit the Author Profile page at Harlequin.com.

CAST OF CHARACTERS

Travis Johnson—US Marshal leading a team assigned to protect the witness and sole survivor of a serial killer's rampage. An easy assignment until the witness proves that there's nothing straightforward about this case.

Kiera Connell—Nurse practitioner at the Prairie Seniors' Care Home. She's the only survivor of a serial killer who has terrorized the country over the past year. She claims the killing isn't over, but no one is listening.

James Perez—FBI lead on the case of a serial killer.

Eric Solomon—Accused serial killer awaiting trial.

Serene Deveraux—FBI security expert. She's ready to take on any challenge.

Devon Gawon—US Marshal, part of the team led by Travis, assigned to protect the witness.

Susan Berker—Determined to get back the life she dreamed of.

Reece Blackburn—US Marshal protecting the witness.

Chapter One

Cheyenne, Wyoming
Late spring

Kiera Connell grabbed her bag and headed with a smile to the exit of the Prairie Seniors' Care Home. Few things made her happier than her work here. In fact, she often came in for extra hours beyond those they paid. She supposed it was because of her own lack of family that made being here so special, made her feel so included. She'd lost her mother when she was a toddler and the aunt who had raised her had died seven years ago. The seniors and the other care-givers were, to her, like family. Today, she'd filled in on an earlier shift before working her scheduled evening shift. It was late, and her car was in for repairs. It was a nice night and only a twenty-minute walk home. She planned not to waste any time getting out the door.

Her hand was on the knob when a quavering voice stopped her.

"Kiera? Do you have a minute?"

She turned around without hesitation. "Sure, Ann," she said. She guessed that the elderly woman had hurried down the hall after her as fast as her walker would take her. Kiera must have been caught up in her own thoughts, for she hadn't heard the shuffle of Ann's feet as she had struggled to follow.

"What's up?"

"I wondered if you could pick up a magazine for me tomorrow."

"I will," Kiera said as she put a reassuring hand on her arm. She'd promised she'd run the errand for her only an hour ago. She'd also promised an hour before that. But Ann, like many of the other residents, had dementia. "I'll get one with racy pictures."

Ann smiled. "You're a tease," she replied. "But thank you."

"I'll see you tomorrow," Kiera promised. "Now get some sleep."

After watching Ann turn slowly around and make her way painfully down the hallway, she headed for the exit. But she glanced back and saw Ann take a wrong turn to get to her room. It was a simple setup, a small facility, but for someone with memory loss, nothing was simple.

Kiera dropped her bag and hurried down the hall. She could leave Ann to find her way to her room on her own. She knew that she would eventually get there. For one corridor only met another and circled back to the starting point. She could wait and let the plan of the hallways take Ann the long route back to where she wanted to go. But she couldn't do that.

It wasn't in her nature. She slowed her step as she walked beside the woman. She chatted to Ann about her day, her plans for tomorrow and the promised magazine. It was a conversation she'd had three other times since supper. Once, when she'd brought Ann's medication. Once, when she made sure that she was ready for bed and again when she checked on her later in the evening. She'd completed the same ritual for half a dozen other people as well, but Ann was one of her favorites. While some of the work was repetitive, it was the people that made this job one of the best she'd ever had. As a nurse-practitioner, it was her that the staff turned to when health issues cropped up. She loved the challenge of keeping this community of seniors healthy. She loved it every bit as much as she loved being part of their support structure.

"Kiera," her supervisor, Beth, called as she left Ann in her room and headed back down the corridor. "What are you still doing here?"

"I was delayed."

"Ann again?" Beth shook her head and smiled. There was no danger of Ann overhearing their almost maternal hovering; she'd disappeared into her room. And, like many of the residents, she was hearing impaired. "I could have given her a hand."

"I know," Kiera replied. "But I was here so..." The words trailed off as she shrugged. She looked at her watch. It was almost midnight.

"Are you sure you don't want to take a cab home?" Beth asked. "It's late."

"I'll be fine. It's a warm night and a short walk."

"Be careful," Beth warned with a wave.

She gave a wave back and headed out the door. It was a beautiful late spring night. She was walking down well-lit streets in an area of the city where she'd always felt safe. The air seemed to caress her skin. She walked by one of the city's eight-foot-tall, artist-painted, decorative cowboy boots. A streetlight splashed light on the gold-and-brass spur and revealed a cloud-studded, bright blue Wyoming sky above a mountain range. The beautiful scene was painted on the body of the boot. The boots were all unique and were displayed randomly throughout the city. They were one of the many things that made Cheyenne special to her. Tonight, this one marked the halfway point, ten minutes from home.

She began to hum a little tune. And, as she walked by a local coffee shop, she noticed a man sitting slouched on an outside bench. It wasn't unusual to see the occasional homeless person in the area, especially during the warmer weather. She thought nothing of it and instead considered jogging the rest of the way home.

"Miss."

The soft male voice came out of nowhere and startled her. But there was no threat in the voice, only a kind of lost hopelessness. She'd heard that tone before. The streetlight pushed the shadows away as another man in a ragged T-shirt and baggy jeans rose from the sidewalk where he'd been sitting cross-legged with cup and a sign asking for help.

He approached her slowly, with a slight limp.

"I'm sorry," he said in a soft voice. "Could you spare some change?"

"Of course," she said and reached into her pocket and pulled out some coins. She dropped them into the cup. He looked thin and grubby. She guessed he might be in his late twenties but not much older. It wasn't a sight that she was unfamiliar with. Occasionally, she volunteered at a nearby soup kitchen. There, she often saw people like him who were homeless or just down on their luck. She sometimes wondered what had brought them to such a desperate state. Whatever the reasons, she couldn't turn down someone in need.

"Have a coffee on me."

He nodded. But it was as if his interest was elsewhere. She turned in the direction that seemed to have caught his attention. And as she turned, she saw the hooded figure approaching. They were alone; the man on the bench had disappeared as if sensing trouble. There was no time to run. There was no time to scream. It was over before she knew that it had happened.

When she opened her eyes again, her arms and shoulders ached. The breeze that had lifted her hair earlier, and which she'd taken joy in walking in, was gone. She was no longer on the street but in what seemed to be a house. Everything was dimly lit, and she could see the shadowy shape of the room: large, empty and rather rank smelling. Her wrists and ankles were tied with rope that was so tight it cut into her skin.

Escape.

And yet, as much as she knew that she needed to get away, she couldn't. Even without the ropes that restrained her, her body was weak and didn't seem to want to respond. Her head spun. She guessed that she might have a concussion. The smell of must and disuse closed around her. Her heart pounded so hard that her chest hurt.

Stay calm, she told herself as she took deep breaths. *That's the only way you're going to figure a way out of this.* But her head reeled, and she passed out. When she came to, everything was dark. She lay still, trying to figure out where she was, who had done this to her and what they wanted. She had to clear her mind. She had to still her fear so that she could think straight. She was focusing like she'd never done before. Hours of yoga, of meditation, were being used in a way she had never thought possible. As soon as she cleared her mind, she realized that, again, she wasn't alone. She could smell rank body odor. She cringed and waited for what might come next.

"I'm going to enjoy every minute with you."

The voice came out of nowhere, sliding through the darkness like a stream of venom.

Kiera thought she might throw up. She held back a shudder.

She knew that voice. It was the homeless man who had asked her for money. That seemed both forever and only minutes ago. Time was lost to her. Her head spun as he whispered a long litany of sexual pleasures he would demand from her. She could smell something rancid on his breath that made her stomach twist and bile rise in her throat. His finger ran along her arm and she held back a shudder. Instinct told her that fear would entice him. Show no fear was second only to escape.

"And then," he said, drawing his words out as if he were about to offer her a unique treasure. "When I am through with you, you will die."

She'd never been more terrified. He didn't need ropes or restraints of any sort—she couldn't have moved if she'd wanted to. It was as if she were part of a TV program. It was as if everything that happened was part of that program, part of that fantasy. She'd wake up soon and it would all be over. A silent shiver crawled through her. This was real life. A nightmare.

"Not until I have my turn."

Kiera didn't know who or what they were, or if the voice was male or female. She only knew that the second voice made her skin crawl.

They moved away from her. Now their voices were low, too low to hear. She passed out again after that. When she awoke, she sensed that she was alone. Time passed. It was broken only by changes in her consciousness. There were moments that she fought with her restraints. There were moments where she drifted back into unconsciousness. In the moments she was conscious, she lived in a state of panic where she feared she would die.

The next time consciousness returned she was aware of a painful ache in her hands. The pain came from lack of circulation, for not only were her wrists tied, but she'd been partially lying on her hands. She shifted, taking the weight of her body off her hands. Something smelled different, a scent that was heavier, like pine and mold strung together. And there was the sense that she'd been moved. She pushed her hands against what felt like a wooden wall and moved them up as high as she could reach. Then, she rolled away from the wall and pain shot through her legs as her fingers touched another wall. Wherever she was, she was in a place much different from the cavernous room she'd first been in. She guessed the size by feel, determining that she had about a foot of space in either direction. As she rolled over again, she could feel wood against her lower back and against her legs. It felt like it was touching her skin, but she'd been wearing pants and a tunic. The only bare skin was her arms, at least that was the way it had been. Kiera felt with her fingers along her leg and felt skin rather than cloth. Further exploration told her that there were large tears in her pants and in her tunic.

Her clothes were torn but still there. She felt in the darkness as surprise ran through her. Considering what had happened, what she'd heard, this wasn't what she'd anticipated. Something had changed, and she didn't know what. She remembered the threats. She knew where this was going. They were frightening her, dragging things out. It was clear in the things they'd said. They wanted her terrified and they'd accomplished that. That they wanted to rape her wasn't in doubt. Their words only confirmed that, but for some reason that hadn't happened. Not yet.

She didn't know why but for now she'd been lucky. But she sensed that time was running out.

There was only one option: she had to get out of here, get away from them before the worst happened. She didn't want to contemplate, again, what that might be. But the possibilities of worst were engraved in her tortured mind. Rape, as they'd promised, or worse—she took a deep, almost panicked breath—death.

The taste of dust and disuse was in her mouth as she began to chew at the rope that bound her wrists. Minutes passed. It could have been hours. Time blended into itself and had no meaning. All she had was hope and she needed to cling to that. Desperate, she tried to pull her wrists apart. Something seemed to give but the rope didn't break.

Kiera rolled over and something sharp bit into her skin. She felt for it awkwardly, twisting her body to get more reach. Something pierced her finger and she bit back a cry of pain but continued her exploration and discovered a nail jutting about a half inch out of the wood. Excitement raced through her. Finally, a tool to free herself. She shimmied closer and began to rub the rope that was binding her wrists against it. Minutes passed and then, the rope snapped. The force of it had her falling backward, missing the nail that had freed her and hitting her head against the wall. She lay like that for seconds as she caught her breath. Then she began to shake her wrists, trying to return circulation to her numb hands. But as blood began to flow, the pain overwhelmed her. She cradled her hands and had to bite her lip to stop from crying out.

Silence and darkness crowded around her. As she lay waiting for the pain to dissipate, a thin stream of light flicked across the room and then disappeared as quickly as it appeared. Her heart leaped. Was it possible that the light came from outside? Where else would it come from? Was it the headlights of a car? Was she near a street or was it just her captors turning a light on and off in another room? The light had appeared to move before it disappeared. Its very presence suggested a possibility. Her heart pounded at the first sign of hope before she struggled to her feet. She felt in the darkness a little over four feet above the floor where the light had seemed to come from. The wall felt different. The wood wasn't as solid and seemed out of line with the rest of the wall. It was a subtle difference, but enough to hint that it might cover something. Her heart raced at what this might mean. She began to pick at the wood. She scratched and clawed with her fingernails and was surprised when a piece broke off easily as if it was not only thin but rotted. Determined, she dug harder. In places the wood was almost like butter while in others it was hard and resistant. Splinters dug into her skin, embedding under her nails. The pain made her eyes water. She didn't stop. Her gut screamed one thing. This was her chance to live.

The wood chipped away piece by piece, sliver by sliver. Now she didn't think of the pain or of the warm trickle that ran down her fingers, and then down her wrists. Vaguely, she knew it was blood. She knew that she was bleeding. It didn't matter. For she knew now, what she'd only guessed before, there was a window behind the wood covering.

The possibility of freedom began to appear as she could see vague shapes, enough to figure that she was looking at an alley. Now half of the window was uncovered. It was enough. She ripped her already torn pants off at the knee and wrapped the material around her hand. Her body shook with stress, with anticipation. She took a deep breath and hauled her arm back. She drove her fist through the window with all the strength she had. The glass shattered. She could feel the slick warmth of blood as it ran down her arm. She forced her mind to think of only one thing—escape. With that thought, she yanked out two more pieces of glass, clearing the bottom half of the window enough so that she could get out.

Freedom.

Kiera sank to the floor and began untying the rope that bound her ankles. She looked up often, her heart pounding. She feared that her captors would burst in at any moment. They'd punish her for what she'd done— kill her even. It wasn't a thought she could entertain. She couldn't think of that. There was no time to speculate.

Finally, she pulled the last knot free and stood up.

There was a sense that time was slipping away. There were furtive noises on the other side of the wall, the one to the right of the window she'd just uncovered. She had to go now. And even though she wasn't a big woman, she knew it would be a tight squeeze. Seconds later, one leg was outside; a breeze ran across her skin and she barely acknowledged that. The jagged edges of glass that she hadn't been able to clear away ripped the places where her skin was bare. The pain only reminded her to keep going, that she wanted to live.

The night air was heaven as it sent goose bumps across her exposed flesh. Her heart raced. Her captors could be anywhere. They could be behind her now.

Kiera flipped over so that she was on her back and didn't land on her head into the unknown darkness. But, with the majority of her body out, she lost her grip. She landed on a pile of plastic garbage bags that broke her fall. For seconds, she lay there, shocked, terrified and exhilarated all at once.

Freedom at last.

Something sharp bit into her side as she struggled to her feet and pain shot through her. Finally, she stood in the darkness shaken and disorientated. She took a breath and then another. And she told herself that if she ever got out of this, if she were truly free, she'd be setting up a safe-ride program for all the workers at the care home.

A streetlight glimmered in the distance. She limped as fast as she could toward the light, and the possibility of freedom.

Cheyenne, Wyoming
One week later

US MARSHAL TRAVIS JOHNSON knew that he should be looking forward to the low-key case he'd just been presented with, especially after his last assignment. It had been high-octane from beginning to end as they'd cornered a drug lord who had made it through two international borders and numerous state lines. But, the truth was, he loved action and he loved a challenge.

"I've received notice that Kiera Connell was discharged from the hospital yesterday." The look James Perez, the FBI lead on this case, gave him was grave.

Travis nodded. He knew the case. He knew that the woman was the only survivor of a serial killer who had terrorized women from coast to coast for well over a year.

"She's safe but we're afraid she might run if she feels otherwise. At this point, no need of twenty-four-seven protection, just a presence that gives her a sense of security. I want you to head the team that will protect her." James shrugged with a half smile. "I wouldn't dump this on you, but considering the high-profile status of this case, we need the best protecting her."

"No worries," he said. He wasn't surprised that James had considered the pressure this might put on him. James was one of the most considerate men he knew. They'd known each other for years, worked together many times, and had eventually become friends who shared many interests including a mutual love of baseball.

"You read the file?"

Travis nodded. He'd followed the case over the past year. The file had only sharpened the details.

"Yeah, I did," he said with a grimace. It didn't matter how long he was in law enforcement, or how many cases he saw, the depths of mankind's depravity could still surprise him. "There appears to be no connection between the witness and killer."

"There isn't, at least that we know. I doubt that will change. From everything the witness said, she's never seen him before."

"That seems to be the usual for this killer. Picks random women," Travis said grimly. Eleven women had died at this man's hands and other than the fact that they were female and attractive, there were no other commonalities. They ranged in age from twenty to forty, their ethnic roots as varied as their ages.

"As you know, she was found here." James turned his computer around. He pointed it out on the detailed map of one of the most neglected areas of the city. "Five o'clock in the morning, a transit driver on her way to work found her. She called it in immediately and stayed with the victim until police and an ambulance arrived."

"A Good Samaritan."

"I salute them almost every day on this job," James said with sincerity.

Travis couldn't agree more. The unsung heroes. The civilians who went above and beyond were an invaluable resource that often went unpraised and unnoticed.

"She was damn lucky," Travis said. Having her alive and able to ID the killer was a huge break in a case that, as horrific as it was, unfortunately, was titillating. The media had had a field day following the trail of the killer and that news had gained a growing body of followers over the months of the spree. Now those killings were being tied to others hinting that the killer might have been active much longer than authorities had known. That was the dark side of humanity. They loved tragedies and horrors, as long as they had no personal connection to them, of course. He pushed the chair back and stood up. Despite what he'd said, he was anxious to get back into action even if it was as non-challenging as babysitting a potential witness who was no longer in danger. The perp had been put behind bars.

"She was lucky. She escaped before she could be assaulted or worse. According to what she told authorities, she wasn't sexually assaulted. She was backhanded a number of times. She has some fairly serious bruising on her left cheek."

Travis swore at the thought of it even though he knew that in the scope of things, that assault was minor.

"Unfortunately, that wasn't the worst this piece of sludge did to other women. Besides the concussion, she has dozens of wood splinters in her hands—and yet none of that stopped her from getting away."

He pushed the file at Travis. "She's spent more time in the hospital for psychiatric evaluation than anything else."

A phone rang.

Travis looked at the picture on the file as James took the call. The dark-haired beauty who had smiled with lighthearted innocence for the photo was frozen in a moment in time when she couldn't imagine the nightmare that was to follow. Since the picture was taken, she'd come close to death. The thought made him feel slightly sick.

"Just a heads-up," James said as he put the phone aside. "She's insistent that she return to work as soon as possible."

"What?"

He looked up, shocked that that would even be a consideration after everything she'd been through.

"I've suggested at least a two-to-three-weeks' wait on that."

Travis said nothing. There was nothing to say, for in reality, he had no say. It was up to the FBI. For him it was an assignment, nothing more. The only thing he knew was that everything about this case was troubling.

Her attacker, Eric Solomon, the man now known as a serial killer who had silently hunted, killed and raped women across the country, was behind bars. Something about the emergency call had triggered an instinctive reaction by the detective in charge that night. He'd felt something off and deployed unmarked vehicles without sirens or flashing lights. The victim had been taken to the hospital while officers had converged quietly on the deserted house where the victim claimed she'd been held. The perpetrator had been caught when he'd returned minutes later and had been unprepared for what awaited him. There, the baby-faced man had been surprised by the police presence. He'd turned to run and been caught and arrested on the spot. The evidence had almost been too easy. The victim's DNA was lodged under his fingernails and strands of her long hair were twisted around his ring finger like a trophy. Once the victim had identified him in a lineup of photos, it was clear that they had their man. He was now awaiting trial.

"In all my years, I've never dealt with this kind of situation," James said. "The perp is behind bars and the victim is still terrified for her life. She thinks there's another killer out there."

"Could it be a delusion brought on by post-traumatic stress?"

"We're definitely considering that possibility. In fact, that is why she was held in the hospital a day or two longer than necessary," James said. "Right now, as you know, our biggest concern is that she might be saying one thing and planning another. I think her talk of going back to work is only a ploy to let us believe she's alright. Truth is, I think she's far from it."

James glanced at his phone as it dinged a message and pushed it away. "I've never seen a victim escape something as dire as she did in quite the way she did. She has a mind of her own and where that might lead her…" He leaned forward. His blue eyes stood out more than usual against his tan complexion. "I can't take any chances with this. We need her on the stand. But…" He paused. "This witness appears to have more guts than any I've seen before."

Travis had to agree with that. For the woman had literally clawed her way out of a closet and broken out through a boarded-up window by crawling through an impossibly small opening. Then, she'd run barefoot down a dark, neglected alley to safety. And when she'd been brought in, James had told him how deadly calm she'd been. There had been no tears or hysterics, only a shaky voice as she'd reported what happened. The tears had come later according to hospital staff but even then, there'd been few. According to the file, and James had confirmed it, she'd been solid in her testimony that would incriminate the perpetrator of one of the worst serial killer rampages the country had seen in recent years. She was a five-star witness and had identified Eric Solomon from a picture lineup presented to her while she was still in the hospital. But there was only one glaring glitch, and it was the fact that she claimed to have heard two voices—both she believed to be men and both with the intent to hurt her. That belief was a glitch that cast a shadow on both her stability and her believability. It was her insistence, with a complete lack of supporting physical evidence, that the killer hadn't worked alone.

Chapter Two

The covers were twisted, some on the bed, some off. The room was still in darkness as Kiera fought with a sheet and finally reached over and flipped on the bedside light. She'd thought she'd heard a sound, something out of the ordinary. Seconds passed. She clutched the sheet as the fridge fan clicked on. The soft whirring seemed loud in the night silence.

"It's the fridge," she muttered as if saying those words would reassure her, as if they would change everything.

It was her second night back in her own home, in her own bed. It had been over a week since the attack. When she'd been discharged from the hospital, she'd been more than ready to pick up her life where it had left off. Except, that wasn't the way it was. The condo she called home no longer felt like one. The funky, crafty style she'd created by shopping flea markets and craft sales, the style that had felt so completely her and so homey, felt foreign. She'd been on edge since she'd come home. And a police officer had been assigned to patrol her area. He made a regular pass of her property, checking in often and would continue, the officer had assured her, until a US marshal took over. While she wasn't under twenty-four-hour surveillance, she was promised a patrol car in her neighborhood and a regular check-in.

She grabbed the book she was reading and her blanket. After heading to the kitchen to start the coffee maker, she curled up on the couch while it brewed. But the cozy mystery lay unopened on her lap despite the fact that it was one that she'd anxiously been waiting to read. She sat quietly, trying to think of anything but the trauma she'd endured.

She looked over at the half-grown cat she'd so recently taken in. Her name was Lucy. Both the name and her reason for being here were fate more than choice. She'd taken the cat so one of the residents at the home where she worked wouldn't lose contact with her pet and would still be able to see her. Now the adolescent cat was curled up on her raspberry-and-blue flowered armchair. Lucy had claimed that chair from the minute she'd been brought home. Kiera stood up and went to sit on the edge of the chair and ran her fingers through Lucy's soft fur. The cat batted at her hand and curled up tighter, presenting her with her back.

"You win," she said with a smile and went back to the couch. But, despite the cat's rejection, it felt good to have her here, to have another living being sharing her space. In fact, she'd picked the cat up from her friend's house the minute she'd been discharged from the hospital. But she knew that she needed more than Lucy to move past the trauma. She needed to dive back into the work she loved. Returning to her routine would get rid of the fear and uncertainty that had rooted in the midst of her life like a field of thistles. Even now, she missed her colleagues' banter and the everyday comings and goings of the care home. The thought of that brought a touch of normalcy to the sense of unreality she'd had since she'd been kidnapped.

She stood up, paced and then sat down again. She knew that the experts disagreed with that theory. They thought that counseling sessions and rest were the answer. She didn't need counselors or psychiatrists or any other health professional to talk her into wellness. What she needed, besides her life back, was to know that both her kidnappers were behind bars. That would make her feel so much better than any therapist ever could. But the authorities thought they had her attacker. No one believed that there were two involved in the attack for there was no physical evidence. Instead, the FBI had assigned a team of marshals to protect her. They weren't here yet, and secretly she felt that they were putting them in place more to ensure that she didn't skip town than to protect her. It was a feeling based on the way they'd phrased things as they laid their protection plan out to her. Whatever they thought about that—they were wrong.

It was five minutes to five o'clock.

The phone rang.

"It's a prank," she muttered. "Someone with a

sick sense of humor." That's what the police officer had said when she'd told him that she'd gotten two calls early yesterday morning. One a hang up and the second heavy breathing. He hadn't taken the calls seriously at all. In fact, he'd called the incidents unfortunate and bad timing, following so closely on the heels of all she'd been through.

Yet, in her heart she didn't believe any of that. Her gut knew it would happen again and her hand shook as she answered.

"Hello," she said and fought to keep the tremor from her voice. "What do you want?"

She was talking to dead air. They'd hung up just as they'd done yesterday at exactly this time.

If they followed yesterday morning's pattern, they'd call again. In exactly ten minutes.

She hit End and wished that she could hurl the phone across the room.

She got up, dropping the blanket and the book on the couch as she went into her bedroom and over to the nightstand. She hesitated a second before opening the drawer. She looked at the gun lying there as if that would somehow make her feel better. The gun had rested in the bottom of her aunt's purse for forty years, or so the woman who had raised her had claimed. She'd kept the gun after she had died, as a memento, nothing more. She didn't like guns. And, for the longest time, aside from getting a permit to carry a concealed weapon, she'd kept it in a locked storage box. Despite the promise of police surveillance, being checked in on didn't feel like it was enough. In her fear, she'd taken the gun out of the locked storage box the day after she left the hospital. Her life had turned on its head. Her aunt had been right, one should always be prepared. If she'd had the gun with her that fateful night, maybe she would never have been taken.

"Auntie Nan, you may have known what you were talking about," she said. Her voice was soft, reflective. She looked upward as if somehow, somewhere, her aunt would be listening.

"Damn it." She hated this, hated the fact that her life was in shreds and now she was the victim of some idiot. A prank caller on top of everything else was too much. For she knew her freedom would soon be curtailed by personal protection. A man prowling her property night and day was not something she wanted, and not, according to the FBI, anything she could avoid.

A US marshal was security she didn't need. They'd soon be here anyway. What she wanted hadn't seemed to matter in over a week. First the kidnapping and now in its aftermath, the surveillance, protection they liked to call it. Despite their insistence of vigilance, the irony was their reasons for it. They didn't believe her claims that there was another killer. Instead, they feared that she would run. There was no danger in either option. She wouldn't run and there was another killer. But Cheyenne wasn't a place where a serial killer could continue his sick activities and not get caught. It wasn't a place where he could blend in. It was a small city and that made it difficult to hide.

Whoever the second killer was, he'd follow a pattern already established over the last year and head to a larger center where there was more opportunity. She was as sure of that as she was that the second killer existed. She tried to tell herself she was safe, that the fact that only one killer was behind bars, didn't matter. She tried to tell herself that the killer that authorities insisted didn't exist, was no threat to her but they would be a threat to another woman in some other town or city in this country. But despite thinking that, she wasn't so sure that she was safe or, that it was over. She wasn't a forensic expert or a psychiatrist, but she knew a little about serial killers. She'd met one face-to-face and she'd been in the presence of the other.

The other. She shuddered for it was the thought of that—of the one on the loose that terrified her most.

The one they hadn't caught, the one they didn't believe in, that one had been the leader. At least, that's what she sensed. She also sensed that nothing would stop them. They'd go on, find a new partner, maybe work alone. But the end result would be that someone else would die. She shuddered. Someone had to stop the killing and to do that someone had to believe her.

At five minutes after five o'clock in the morning, the phone rang again. There was no point hesitating. That wouldn't make any of this go away. She answered.

The deep breathing started. As it had before, it went on for a minute. This time she said nothing after the first hello, not for thirty seconds. Then she demanded that this end. She demanded an identity. She got neither of her demands. The phone call ended exactly thirty seconds after that.

She tossed the phone to the other end of the couch as if distance would make a statement, end the harassment. Prank calls were what she had thought yesterday. But now she sensed something else was at play, as a sense of déjà vu almost choked her.

THE SUN HAD only begun to rise when Travis turned the corner onto the quiet residential street. The assignment was low-key. That's what he'd thought going in. He'd also learned a long time ago that situations like this could turn on a dime. And a second read of the file gave him a feeling that something was off. It was because of that, because he trusted his instincts, that he was here this early. His shift didn't start for another three hours. Something told him that he needed to be more proactive than normal.

He wanted to get a clear handle on things. He wanted an uninterrupted look at what he was dealing with. That included not only the witness but her environment as it was now—undisturbed. Less than a minute later, he pulled up to the three-story off-white condo building in the middle of the block. The ground-floor unit was the one that the witness, Kiera Connell, resided in. She'd purchased it a year ago. He knew that because he'd already run a check on the property. It was built five years ago, and she was the second owner. They were trivial facts but even in a low-threat case like this, it was his habit to research such things. Even though there was a driveway, he parked the SUV in the parking lot a group of similar buildings shared. It was too early in the morning to knock on her door and introduce himself. The entire building, including her condo, was still in darkness. He could see the darker shadows of flowers in the flower bed. Everything seemed to be in place—neat and organized.

He wondered what the inside of her place was like and he wondered what the occupant was like. He didn't know what she'd been like before the incident. But he could only guess that now she would be in need of support and counseling for many months, or even years, to come. She'd survived a vicious attack by a serial killer who had left a trail of women dead. The women had all been raped and then murdered, all except the first two. They'd been murdered without any evidence of sexual assault. That wasn't odd but rather an indicator that the perpetrator had evolved. An attack like that could leave the victim broken and unable to return to their former life. He hoped that wasn't the case. But the law of averages wasn't in her favor. It was too bad. According to the file, she'd been a determined young woman. She had carved a career for herself despite adversity. But a file never told the whole story, nor did the authorities who led the investigation. To keep her safe, he needed to know who she was as a person. That was for later; for now he'd scout out the area. The advantage of this early hour was that he could do so without any distractions. He was lead on the team of marshals who would protect Kiera Connell. The danger to the witness was minimal. Despite the low risk of danger, he was working the case like he did any other.

On this assignment, he'd had shorter notice than most. It was up to him and his team to keep her safe and make sure she kept it together until the trial was over. The feds had pinned their case not only on the evidence they'd collected but on the testimony of the only witness.

He'd learned as much as he could about the woman who was his latest assignment. It fascinated him that she was the only victim who had escaped. That a twenty-five-year-old nurse, with little life experience, had been the one to do it—that, to him, was mind-blowing. Although, he couldn't imagine how messed up she must be from the experience at the madman's hands. He felt for her. But he still would rather bow out of this assignment. For, he saw little challenge. The perp was behind bars and he and his team were effectively babysitters to a witness who was too important for authorities to take any chances on. She was the key to ending a killing spree that had lasted far too long. For they suspected it had gone on long before they'd become aware of it. All that aside, bowing out was, unfortunately, not an option.

He looked at his watch. It was twenty to six. He'd been up since four after only five hours of sleep. It wasn't a big sleep loss, only an hour less than he usually got. He shrugged the thought away. It wasn't a factor. The amount of time that had passed since he'd arrived was. He'd learned a long time ago that time could slip away if not tracked and organized. Time was critical for it could mean life or death. That was why he always kept a tight schedule and a close eye on the time.

A window at the front of her property was open a crack. It was the swing-out kind that, if one was into such things, could open from the outside. He frowned at that. No matter that the killer was behind bars—open windows low to the ground were begging for a crime to happen. He stood at the corner of the condo. The sun was rising. Streaks of sunlight were making it easy to see without the aid of a flashlight. He took a step forward meaning to scout the entire perimeter of the unit.

"Freeze! Take one more step and I'll shoot."

The woman's voice came out of nowhere. He'd been broadsided. *Damn it*, he thought. He'd been caught with his pants figuratively down. He turned and saw out of the corner of his eye the barrel of a handgun. He didn't dare turn right around, even though he wanted to. But he didn't plan to die today, or any day in the immediate future.

"Drop your weapon!"

There was no way in hell that was happening. His mind ticked through the options. He could take her down, but he had to get closer. He hoped her attention was on his weapon as he dropped it to his side, still holding it in his left hand. At the same time, he took a step backward, toward her.

"Do it!" she snapped. "And don't take another step."

"I'm a US—"

"I don't care who you are," she interrupted. "Put your hands where I can see them and drop your gun."

He slid his gun into his holster and lifted both hands in the air. He had his badge in one hand, having pulled it out from the side of his holster as he'd holstered the gun. "I'm going to toss my badge—"

"No!" she interrupted. "You'll throw nothing."

Damn it, he thought again. He was furious with himself. She'd snuck up on him. But she hadn't come out of nowhere. He should have sensed that he wasn't alone. He should have known. *Hell,* he thought. He should have expected it, been prepared for it. It was the basic tenet of any scout pack—Be Prepared— never mind a US marshal. He'd missed the signs that she was near. And because of that, he was at the wrong end of a gun. Was he getting old? His friends had teased him about that only a week earlier over a couple of beers. They'd been celebrating his thirtieth birthday. He discounted that thought. He worked hard to be at the top of his game. Still, that didn't change the fact that he'd screwed up—big time.

"Who are you?" he asked. If nothing else, he deserved to know who was threatening him. More important, he needed to put himself back where he belonged, in charge of this situation.

She fired a shot that kicked up dirt two feet to his right.

"What the hell!" he roared and almost spun around, stopping himself with sheer willpower.

"Another word and you're a dead man," she retorted.

A thought came to him that was as outrageous as

it was possible. After all, it was her condo that he was standing outside. The more he thought it, the more the idea gained plausibility. Was it possible that this was the witness he'd come to protect?

"I'm here to—"

"Do you not understand English? Shut up," she said.

The words were angry and spoken with no hesitation, no hysteria and no tears. That wasn't what he expected if she was the witness. But if it wasn't her, who was she?

"Turn around," she ordered. "And do it slowly."

There was something about her voice. A silken edge that in another time and another place might have been erotic. He couldn't help the thought. It was a voice that could do things to a man in the darkness of the night.

He found it interesting that her voice vibrated a bit as if she was nervous or traumatized. Had she never held a gun before? It was a possibility. And a possibility where he'd been lucky that she hadn't hit him.

He pivoted on a heel. He wanted to give her the impression of how little he cared about her demands, or the fact that she had the advantage. She needed to know that he didn't fear her.

But when he faced her, he could only stare. For the woman holding a gun on him with a grim but determined expression was the face on the witness's file. He was facing the very woman he was to protect, and the file picture had done her no justice. In the picture she'd been pretty; in real life she was so much more than that. The rising sun highlighted her dark hair, giving it a glossy sheen that framed her beautiful face. She was petite, no more than a few inches over five feet. She was slim and yet voluptuous in a way that made him fight to keep his eyes up and on her face. It was an attraction that he hadn't felt in a very long time, if ever. She mesmerized him with a look.

He was pinned by green eyes. They were eyes that would have held him forever if it weren't for the gun that she had yet to lower. The moment shifted everything he knew about this case. A simple, uncomplicated assignment had just become difficult. Difficult in ways he'd never imagined.

Chapter Three

"Kiera Connell?"

"How do you know me?" Kiera's voice cracked as it had off and on since her ordeal. She hoped that it wasn't on the edge of breaking or of her losing it like she had for an hour only yesterday. She couldn't afford to lose her voice when a strange man was roaming her property. After everything she'd been through this was beyond disconcerting. She wanted to ask who he was, why he was here but she feared that her voice wouldn't hold out. That he knew her name was interesting but not startling. There was a list of owners in the common area. The question that was more troubling was—had he been casing the place?

"I don't."

The easy way he spoke combined with his soulful brown eyes seemed to say that none of this bothered him. That this was just an everyday occurrence. Who was he?

He took a step forward.

"Take another step and you die."

It was a stupid thing to say and she knew it. She'd

already threatened him with death once and despite her threats, she doubted if she could kill him. Pull the trigger, yes, she'd already done that. But that had all been for show. If she was going to threaten to kill, she should be able to make good on that threat. She'd only shot the gun at the shooting range and then here, when she'd dusted the top of a dandelion to prove her point. She didn't like the feeling of aiming a killing weapon at another human being, at any being.

"Who are you and what are you doing slinking around my place in the dark?"

Except it wasn't dark anymore. The sun had cleared the night shadows and the neighborhood was coming to life. Soon one of her neighbors would be wondering what was going on. On the upside, she was sure that if someone were to see their little tableau, they would be quick to call the police. This wasn't the kind of neighborhood where guns and violence were common. In fact, she'd never seen or heard of an incident in the time she'd been here.

"Travis Johnson…" He broke off as if reconsidering saying anything else but instead took a step forward.

"Stop!" Her throat hurt at the effort, but it didn't break. She clenched the gun so tight that her palm was beginning to sweat.

She frowned. He hadn't ditched his gun as she'd demanded, only holstered it. She wasn't sure how she'd let that get past her. She guessed that she would have had to shoot him for him to relinquish the weapon as she'd demanded. Except for the weapon which he was careful to keep his hand away from, he was complying. Not once had he tried to overpower her, to take the gun from her. Considering how fit he looked, she guessed he could have easily been able to overpower her. Instead, he'd let her remain in control, let the situation play out. Except for the gun, none of his mannerisms indicated that he was the trespasser or thief that she'd first thought. His voice was low and calm as if having a gun held to him was a normal way to begin his day. His stance was relaxed, as if she were no threat. That annoyed her.

Despite the discomfort, she held the gun tighter. It was as if by doing that she was safe—protected even more than before. Her eyes met his. His brown eyes were steady and in an odd way honest. Yet something ran under his calm surface. She speculated that he hid a harder, darker side. The thought of that made her hold back a shiver. She needed no more darker sides. She'd faced more darkness than she ever wanted to see in this lifetime. And yet it wasn't over. There was still the trial. And there was still… She pulled her thoughts back from another terrifying reality. One that was hers alone, for no one else believed her.

"Okay, Travis Johnson. Why are you on my property?"

"I'm a US marshal," he said quickly, as if afraid that she was going to cut him off again.

She couldn't hide the look of disbelief on her face. Despite her earlier analysis, there was something about him that made her think of the bad boy in high school and not of someone in law enforcement. Except, this was no boy. He was tall and broad shouldered, with a rough but good-looking face and a tough-as-nails attitude. With the early morning shadows lifted, it was clear that he likely wasn't a common thief. Besides, she doubted if one would be this confident after being caught red-handed trespassing.

"Identification?"

He held out something that glinted in the early morning sun. "My badge."

It looked official enough. And she had been told there would be protection.

"You can call—"

"I don't need you to tell me who I can call," she said and couldn't keep the bite from her words. She didn't like the way he was looking at her. She had too many men look at her like that and the last thing she needed was another. Except if she were honest, there was no lust in his eyes, only an intense determination. She didn't like that either.

Despite that, she lowered the gun. She held it stiff and inches away from her hip. "So, you're the protection I was promised."

"Yes," he said. "Along with two other US marshals. We are your security team from now through the trial." He shifted as if contemplating moving a step closer.

"Don't move," she demanded.

"I have to say I've never had a witness react like this before," he said looking down at the lowered gun.

"I'm betting that you've never met someone who escaped a serial killer either," she said. She couldn't help herself. Even in this situation she wasn't about to take guff from anyone. She told it like it was; she always had.

"No." He shook his head. "You're right. You're the first." He took a step forward, his hand out. She held out her hand and noticed that he had to reach and take a step forward to accept it. She hated her small size in a situation like this for it made her feel at a disadvantage. He took her hand and it seemed to be swallowed in his as he gave it a firm shake and let go.

"Marshal Travis Johnson. Here to protect you and make sure that your testimony is given, and that piece of trash is put away for good."

There was something in the tone of his voice that held a doubt she couldn't identify, as if he questioned his assignment.

"You think there might be a problem?" she asked.

"No problem," he said. "Look, let's go inside and talk there before you have your neighbors wondering what's going on." He eyed the gun. "You might want to put that away."

"This way," she said and ignored his suggestion as she brushed past him. Their eyes met as she passed. His seemed to see beyond what she'd left unsaid, as if he knew her very thoughts. She looked away. He might be here to protect her, but he had no idea what he was up against. For there was another threat. The fact that it was faceless didn't make it any less deadly.

"Would you like a drink? Water, coffee?" Kiera asked as she closed the back door to her condo.

"Coffee, please."

"Follow me," she said with a no-nonsense tone of voice, as she led the way to the kitchen.

The unit was compact with only one bedroom, a living area and the kitchen. Despite the small space, everything seemed neat and organized. There was a homey feel to the way she'd decorated, and the smell of coffee seemed to permeate everything.

"Have a seat," she said. "I'll just be a minute. I obviously need to put this away." She raised her gun hand mere inches, enough to make it clear that it was the gun she was putting away.

And with that she turned and disappeared into the bedroom. He heard a drawer open and close, and then she returned empty handed and went to the cupboard, pulling out two cups and lifting the coffee carafe and pouring them each a cup.

He felt out of place, too big for the space and very much as though he were intruding. He accepted the coffee cup from her and noticed that her hand shook. He wished there was something he could do to take the fear away from her but knew he had nothing to offer but his presence. Her fears existed in the past and in the unknown of her future.

They sat across from each other and for a minute neither of them said anything. She'd been through hell and he didn't know what he should address first. He ran through a list of things that he knew he needed to ask, to tell her. Where to begin eluded him. When he looked at her he saw the way she rubbed her thumb against the tablecloth and when she looked up, he noticed the whiteness of her lips, and that's when he knew just how much stress she was under.

Another minute went by and the silence was heavier, more awkward.

"I'm glad I have my aunt's gun," she said in a soft voice that broke the silence.

"If you find yourself in a situation in the future where you need to pull a weapon to defend yourself, just remember—you have to be ready to use it." He paused. "You weren't today, were you? I don't count a wild shot, completely off mark, as prepared."

"I don't know, maybe."

"Maybe is as good as no, and in another situation, hesitation would have been fatal—for you."

"Then I can't hesitate."

"Exactly," he said. "On the upside, I'm here to make sure that you never need that gun. If it's not me, it will be another marshal making sure you're safe. Although, we'll need some help from you."

"What do you need?"

"The truth and—" he paused "—your trust. That means that if there's anything you haven't said, anything you're holding off saying, you need to tell me."

"I've already told the FBI everything I know," she said. "And they don't believe all of it."

"Everything?" he asked. He hoped that she'd give him something that could be used in the case. She'd seen one face only and she'd identified him, for now that was what they had to work with.

"He wasn't working alone," she said. "I heard…"

Her voice dropped as his heart sank.

She couldn't repeat this, not in court. It would make her testimony questionable if she spouted those beliefs like facts with no physical evidence to back them up. They needed an ID on a killer, nothing else. Certainly not a belief that had no support, no evidence, no backing of any kind and seemed more fantasy than reality.

"Kiera, we can't assume…"

"Not without evidence," she said with a nod of her head. "I realize that. But there's something else. I don't think it's connected, but it's frightening."

"What's going on, Kiera?" he asked hoping that maybe going along with her might be a better way to eventually get her off this particular track.

"I'm getting anonymous calls," she said. "In the early hours. Yesterday was the first morning I was home since the attack and that's when they started. There was another this morning. They were both the same. The phone rings at five minutes to five o'clock in the morning and then again at five minutes after five."

That much he hadn't heard. Had it been reported? He doubted it, for it was a fairly glaring oversight and James was nothing but thorough. Another thought hit him. He pulled out his phone as he stood up. His knee caught on the table. Coffee slopped from his cup. It just missed the embroidered tablecloth.

"I'm sorry," he said. But he could only think of what she'd said. Five minutes after five o'clock in the morning was the time the 911 call had come in.

The facts from the time she was found and how it had rolled out as the authorities took charge were engraved in his mind. The time of her rescue wasn't public knowledge. He couldn't imagine the time being anything more than a coincidence though. He wasn't sure if even she knew the exact time of her escape. He wasn't sure if anyone had told her. She might only know it was early in the morning, unless she had asked. Either way, he didn't like the sound of any of this. The bus driver who had first found her knew the time, as did the police and the first responders. Would one of them have leaked the information? Except for the bus driver, that would be a breach of confidentiality and mean immediate firing. He made a mental note to mention the possibility that there was a leak to James. The thought, even the possibility, that someone had taken that information and used it to harass her was, to say the least, disconcerting.

She was back with a dishrag in her hand.

"Let me," he said. He took the cloth from her and wiped up the coffee just as it had come close to creeping onto the edges of the tablecloth.

"Got it," he said handing the cloth back. The tablecloth was unique, and he guessed that it was handmade. He'd seen his mother and his aunts embroider many such pieces. This one was a beautiful, vibrant garden scene.

"You embroider?"

"No," she said with a smile. "I found it at a craft sale." She leaned over to take the dishrag and wiped a drop he'd missed.

A minute later she sat down. It seemed that she moved slowly every time she was forced to sit anywhere near him.

"Have you reported the calls?" he asked despite the obvious tension.

"Yes," she said. "Sort of. I spoke to the police officer who was here yesterday but no, unless he put a report forward, which I doubt, they weren't officially reported. I left that to him." She got up as if she was unable to sit, as if his proximity made her nervous.

"Kiera? Are you alright?"

"Would you like more coffee?" she asked with her back to him.

"No thanks. Look, I'm sorry that this is happening. I'm sorry—"

She turned around and there was a pallor to her face. "It's alright. It's me. This is just all so difficult."

He'd taken the wrong approach. He'd been in her face since the beginning, but he wasn't used to dealing with a woman traumatized in quite the way she had been.

"Look, I'll have another cup of coffee, if you'll have one too."

A look of relief crossed her face. And a few minutes later they were talking easily about the craft sales in the area and he was silently thanking the women in his life, in his family, for his knowledge of such things. Ten minutes later she was looking, if not relaxed, at least not so tense that she'd leap at the slightest sound.

"Kiera, I hate to ask this, but you said the anonymous calls you received the last two nights or more specifically, early morning, weren't reported. Why not?"

She shrugged and was quiet for a minute. He gave her time to get her thoughts together and wondered what she was afraid of revealing and why.

"Like I said, I told the police officer the other night, after the first occurrence. He told me there was nothing to be frightened of, that a prank call was just the luck of the draw."

"He brushed them off?" Travis asked as he fought outrage and tried not to let that emotion show in his voice. "You didn't tell him the time and that there were two of them?"

"I told him all of it," she said. "He didn't believe any of it was part of what happened. I don't believe that. Someone needs to know."

Damn it, Travis thought. There'd been no mention of this, no report. Heads would roll. He pushed the anger back and instead focused his attention on her.

"Tell me about the phone calls," he encouraged in a gentler tone.

She looked at him with relief.

"And don't hesitate to tell me anything from here on out."

She nodded and something in the set of her chin seemed less tense.

"The call occurred again this morning. Two calls, two early morning calls in a row. It begins with a ring and a hang up. Then, ten minutes later, five minutes after five o'clock, they call again. The second call is always heavy breathing for about a minute before they disconnect."

He was quiet, considering what she had said.

"Here." She tossed her phone to him. "The calls are there. They're listed as unknown but the time, duration…"

He looked at the phone's history that confirmed what she'd already said, although he'd never doubted her—at least on that fact.

"We may get along yet," she said with a cough. She covered her mouth and turned away. "Excuse me," she said. "How long did you say I was stuck with you and—" she coughed again and then turned, gave a slight smile, as politeness disappeared "—and, as my aunt would have said, your ilk."

"Right until the bitter end, sweetheart," he said, glad to, again, see the hint of attitude. It gave him hope that she'd be able to overcome the trauma she'd endured. She was a strong woman. That was what the therapist had put in his report, and he'd been right. Not many could endure what she had.

"You have no idea what that might mean."

"You'll be safe, I promise," he said although he knew that wasn't what she'd been alluding to but rather the unknown that lay between now and the trial.

"Will I?" she asked.

He looked into her eyes and saw heartbreak and fear. Both were emotions that tore at his heart in a way no woman had affected him in a long time. But she'd been through more than he could imagine. And other than preventing further threats, he couldn't change what had happened. He couldn't stop the fear, for that arose from a horrifying experience that he could not change. He could only hope that his protection made her feel safe despite prank calls in the middle of the night. He could only try his best to help her face the nightmare she'd endured.

"The calls, they're just opportunistic pranks, aren't they?" She asked the question with hope in her voice. She turned away, her shoulders slouched.

"Kiera," he began. "I'm sorry you weren't taken seriously." He thought of the police officer who'd blown the first calls off. He'd be having a few words with him. "They might be pranks." He wanted to say that they also might not. But all of this was guesswork and needed investigation, monitoring. "I'll handle this."

She turned around to face him. "I can't stop thinking about the phone calls and why they chose me, now of all times. My name wasn't made public. It's a stretch to think that there'd be a connection at all. But the time the last one comes in is about the same time in the morning when I was rescued—give or take. I don't know the exact time—I never asked."

He knew the exact time. He also knew that she was right.

It seemed too coincidental. It seemed too everything. Had someone leaked information and this was their idea of a prank? He hoped not. He hoped it was an unfortunate coincidence. If they continued, he'd have her phone rerouted and the calls handled. She needed time to heal and get on with her life. The calls were obviously frightening her, threatening her peace of mind. And, because of that, they had to end.

He stood up. His gut told him that something else was going on, that this case wasn't as straightforward as everyone thought. There might not be a second serial killer, but something was off, something had been missed.

"I'll be doing some back and forth from the office to here. But I'll be available by phone and I'll be in and out throughout the day. There'll never be a moment when you can't reach me or one of my team." Seeing how frightened she looked, he made a snap decision. He would be here for her until daylight tomorrow. "Tonight, if you get any more of these calls, I'll be in my vehicle, in your driveway. Get me."

"I will," she said softly. "That's guaranteed."

But it wasn't her next words so much as the finality with which she said them that, despite what he believed, made his blood chill.

"Whoever wanted me dead. Whoever I escaped from. One of them is still out there."

Chapter Four

Kiera struggled to catch her breath. Her heart pounded so wildly that her chest ached. Her life depended on escape and yet she couldn't move. She was tied, gagged and stuffed into a space so small that when she rolled over she touched a wall on either side. Her legs were numb from lack of circulation. She was trapped and there was nothing but darkness. She didn't know how long she'd been here or how long before it was over. Over— Her heart raced, for that could mean she lived but it could also mean she died. She took a breath. She fought to still her pounding heart. Fought to keep her mind off all the horrible possibilities. She had to keep sane.

KIERA WOKE WITH a gasp. She was sitting up. The sheets were tangled around her. The pillow was on the floor and the quilt had slid off the bed. She gulped air as if she were drowning. Despite her pounding heart she reached for the phone. She knew what happened next, for it had happened before.

But the phone sat cold and silent in her palm. The

phone calls had, in such a short time, become an un-wanted ritual. She looked at her phone. It wasn't time. It was too early for the calls that she had begun to both expect and dread.

She shivered not from cold but from dread. She prayed for this to go away, for the nightmare to end. But no amount of wishing made it go away.

Chills ran down her spine. She grabbed the edge of the quilt and pulled it up and around herself. Despite being well into spring, it was chilly tonight. It was like the weather was a harbinger of more bad luck, as if shadows had poked dark fingers into a life that had once been full of hope and love. It was a life she'd built from the broken fragments of the family she'd lost. It was a life that was hard-won and one she loved. She fingered the edge of the quilt as if that would calm her. But the anticipation of what was to come and what had happened in the too-recent past lay heavily on her.

The bedside lamp sent a warm glow over the quilt. She took deep breaths as she'd learned to do in beginner's level meditation. She'd begun the course weeks ago, when her life had been normal.

Normal.

She tried to concentrate on the quilt and on the vi-brant colors that she'd admired when she'd first seen it at a local craft sale. She ran her thumb back and forth across the finely stitched embroidery. She'd spent hours furnishing and decorating her condo. She'd made it hers with bright pictures and homey touches, like the quilt and the handmade tablecloth that covered her kitchen table. She'd loved her place—it was the first home she'd ever owned, and it was totally hers. But now, she felt as if she sat in the middle of a stranger's things. Nothing gave her solace. Instead, she felt edgy and out of sorts. Almost five minutes to five o'clock in the morning. The phone would ring very soon and as much as she feared that, she feared who it might be more.

Everything she knew about this caller was unprovable. Yesterday she'd taken a chance by telling Travis. Despite saying he would be there for her, she knew that he doubted her claim that the phone calls were tied to the killer she'd escaped. She didn't blame him for doubting. The authorities believed that the killer was behind bars. She'd have been surprised if his reaction had been any different. In a similar situation, she knew she'd do the same. For there was no evidence, no proof of anything, never mind that he had an accomplice.

The phone rang. She didn't dare breathe. Instead, she looked at it as if it were an evil stepsister. She wanted to toss it across the room but that would end none of this. It rang again. And, she knew with a sick feeling, that this was far from over.

She gritted her teeth. Whoever this was, whatever it was, it wasn't going to bring her down. She shivered and hit Answer.

"Hello?"

Silence.

"Answer me, damn it."

The call ended.

She wanted to pitch the phone across the room. Instead, she set it down. But she knew that in ten minutes, if it followed the pattern of the last few nights, the phone would ring again. She tried to calm herself by remembering what Travis had said and remembering the fact that he was still here, just feet away. She'd invited him inside but he'd refused.

She stood looking out her living room window. Her front yard was shrouded in darkness. She wondered if there was someone out there, waiting in the dark. An entity more terrifying even than what she had escaped—out there and still looking for her. She pushed the thought away and looked to her left. There, she could see the shadow of Travis's SUV. Somehow, knowing he was there made her feel safe but didn't remove her dread as she waited for what would come next.

She wished that she could believe the authorities, believe that she was safe. She wished that she could believe that no more women would die. But she wasn't so sure. What she was sure of was that not that long ago she'd had a job she loved, people she cared about and a life. Then everything had changed. She knew it didn't mean that was over. Although she wanted so badly to go back to that, to a normal life, to a place where the nightmare hadn't happened. But she knew that nothing would change what had happened, time would only blunt the brutal memory. Eventually she'd go back to work, to her regular life and to the people she considered friends and family. When she did, she knew it would be different, and eventually she knew that would be okay.

She shuddered and crossed her arms tightly as if that would provide some comfort. She desperately wanted her old life back. She wished that she could hit Restart and go back to the way things used to be. But there was no going back, she'd been through a trauma that had been life changing.

Her testimony, as the only known survivor of a serial killer, would hopefully seal one killer's fate. For now, that had to be enough. It was time to concentrate on her own health, at least that's what the therapist would have her believe. But he was in the same camp as the other authorities. No one believed that there was more than one killer. But she knew that she hadn't imagined the second voice. She knew in her heart that the man who had tried to kill her and, if she hadn't escaped that closet, would have succeeded and left her like almost a dozen other women in a shallow unmarked grave—hadn't been killing alone. But, with no evidence of any of that, her claim was dismissed. Even the therapist had blown it off. He'd stated that she may have suffered an auditory hallucination. He'd come to that conclusion when she had described the second voice as one that she couldn't peg as either male or female but as something distant and sexless. He had then offered a label for the experience. Apparently, what she'd heard was a normal symptom after a trauma like one which she had experienced.

Her mind went back to the call, the one that always followed the first. Her hands shook at the thought.

She had made Travis a promise. She'd promised she'd get him if she had trouble or if she received a phone call where no one answered, as it had in the last two early mornings. Although he didn't believe there was a connection between the phone call and her earlier trauma, she knew that he was here to protect her, to help her even and right now, he was all she had.

She didn't think to grab her robe from the closet. Instead, she padded to the front door in the light shorts and T-shirt she'd slept in, her bare feet quiet against the cool laminate flooring.

She hesitated at the door. Doubts rose and made her rethink her decision. Should she get him—should she leave it? In the scope of what she'd endured, the phone call was nothing. More than likely a prank call as he'd suggested. Before she could decide one way or another, an abrupt knock sounded. She jumped back with an involuntary shriek.

She looked through the peephole.

Travis.

She barely knew him and yet it was like seeing a long-lost friend. She fixated on one important fact; he was on her side. She unlocked the door and stood aside to let him pass. But he didn't. Instead his hands dropped to her shoulders and his eyes were filled with concern.

"What happened?" he asked with a frown. It was as if he already knew. "What's wrong?" He added that question on top of the other when she didn't answer. Without waiting another second, he pulled her into his arms.

It was a friend's hug, one meant to comfort. He was warm and solid against her. And while it lasted only seconds, he was exactly what she needed. It was a promise of protection that no words could offer.

He let her go as he closed the door behind him and stepped farther into the room. She followed. In the space of seconds, everything had changed. And, for the second time in twenty-four hours, she felt protected—safe.

Chapter Five

"Someone called and hung up. I'll be alright," she said before he could say anything.

He wasn't so sure. She'd been pushed to her limits and beyond. No one should have to endure what she had. He wanted to comfort her but there was nothing that he could say that would change what had happened. He could only offer his protection, his words that didn't change anything and his promise to protect.

She shivered in her light T-shirt and shorts.

He glanced to where the afghan hung over the edge of her sofa. She was meticulous about her things. He'd learned that yesterday. The arrangement of her house, the position of her belongings was as familiar as his apartment. Yesterday, he'd made it a point to get to know her environment. Now he knew what might help and what might hinder her, what he needed to know to keep her safe. He went over to the sofa and got the afghan. He brought it back and placed it over her shoulders.

"Thank you," she said as she looked at him with a gentle smile.

"You're welcome," he replied. Even though he wasn't quite sure if she was thanking him for the afghan, for noticing that she was cold—or for being here. Maybe for all three.

"For noticing." She finished on a rather lame note, as if she'd been privy to his thoughts.

He considered asking her to give him her phone, let him take charge. He wasn't sure if she was ready for that.

One thought rolled into the other. He was overthinking it all. Still, he hesitated, unsure for one of the few times in his career. He didn't want to misstep. She was fragile. In a situation like this he knew that, for the victim, control was something that was important, even if it was an illusion. That meant not taking her power away from her. In this case, he decided, she would lead.

"Was it the same as last time?"

"Yes. There was just dead air after I said hello and they hung up within seconds. I didn't say anything more. I don't know why…"

"I'm glad you didn't," he said. He couldn't help himself. He put a hand on her shoulder as his other hand lifted the edge of the afghan that trailed on the floor and wrapped it more securely around her. "That's why I came to your door. I wanted to be here, in case it happened again."

"Thank you."

He tensed. There was a quiver in her voice and

it was hoarse. But when he looked at her, he knew that it wasn't tears that had changed her voice. She was tougher than that. She'd proved that by surviving her ordeal, and by confronting him yesterday. He wanted to lash out at the perpetrator. He wanted to roar with anger but there was nowhere and no one to vent his ire at.

He looked at his watch.

"The next call should be in five minutes," she said as she watched him.

A frown marred her beautiful creamy skin. The lines in her forehead only drew his attention further, to the bruise on her cheek. The bruise was only beginning to yellow. He wanted to reach out and run a thumb along it, to somehow emphasize that it would never happen again, not on his watch. Her kidnapper had backhanded her more than once according to what was reported. Reading that in the file enraged him. Hearing James mention it and now seeing the evidence again only made him want retribution, vigilante justice. None of that would happen.

"You think it will follow the same pattern as the previous nights?" He asked the unnecessary question in an attempt to divert his thoughts.

"Yes," she said, "I don't have any doubt. It's already begun."

He wished there was something he could do to stop the idiot who was doing this. This was a coward at work. A coward who was further scaring a woman who had been terrorized beyond what any human should have to endure. He wanted to get his hands on the piece of crap who was doing this.

The fact that there was nothing he could do only made him feel awkward, and too big for the small living space. The driveway surveillance had been long and monotonous and despite his orders to the other two marshals who would take turns relieving him, that there was no need to remain every minute on location, he'd remained for every hour of his shift and beyond.

His thoughts went back to the possibility of another call, minutes away. Was the caller just picking a random number? Had the caller heard a woman's voice and that had prompted him to continue his rather sick game? Or was this something deadlier, as Kiera had alluded to?

"Have a seat," she said and pointed to the couch that sat angled in a way that offered a view of both the front and back yards.

The condo was small and yet its size was inviting and reflected her personality. They'd talked yesterday beyond the parameters of the case and she'd told him that she loved to sit on the couch and read. The butter-yellow couch was completely her. In a way it seemed to reflect her warm personality. He remembered times through the day when they'd talked about something other than the case. He could see her sitting there in the lazy hours of the evening reading on that same couch. He sat on the left side. She'd already told him that the right-hand side was where she sat. She'd said that with a laugh. They both knew that with her living alone, the whole darn couch was hers, she could sit anywhere, not just on the side she said she claimed. A side she also said she preferred for it allowed her to watch the birds and squirrels come in for the seeds and peanuts that she left out for them.

"It will be okay. I promise, Kiera. The killer is locked up. He can't get to you. The calls are nothing but some jerk with nothing better to do."

"Maybe," she said. But the word held neither sureness nor fear. "But how did they get my number?"

Random chance, the explanation he'd offered when he'd first heard of the calls, hadn't sounded plausible even to his own ears. It hadn't yesterday either. He wasn't sure what the connection could possibly be. The serial killer was behind bars unable to perpetrate such calls. Possibly, someone with an evil bent. He was at a loss.

Two minutes to go.

"When you answer, put your phone on Speaker," he said as he handed the phone to her.

"I will," she agreed.

Another minute ticked by. She looked at him but didn't say anything. He'd protected other witnesses, especially in his early days as a US marshal, but none who had gone through what she had. It enraged him to think about what had been done, what she'd escaped.

She looked at him with fear in her eyes and a tense, determined look to her lips.

It was four minutes after five o'clock.

"I'm here, Kiera. It will be alright. We'll put an end to this, I promise." He squeezed her hand and she held on tight as if she never wanted to let go.

Chapter Six

At exactly five minutes after five o'clock in the morning, the phone rang just as Kiera had said that it would, just as she said it had every early morning since she'd left the hospital.

She held the phone and looked at him. "Answer?" she asked and the hand holding the phone trembled.

"Answer," Travis said without hesitation and only assurance in his voice.

But she seemed frozen, her face pale. The phone rang again.

"I'm right here," he reminded her. "Answer."

She hit Answer with a trembling finger. Despite her earlier reaction, her hello was impressive in its control. He reached over and hit Speaker.

Heavy breathing, steady, rhythmic. There was a hoarse edge to the breathing like someone with a respiratory problem.

Her face was stiff, masklike. She held the phone away from her and touched it only with her fingertips, as though it was poisonous.

He reached over and took it from her. The heavy

breathing was slow and drawn out and carried on for another few seconds. Then silence.

One second, two.

Travis let it play out, let the caller lead. Finally, the silence ended with a raspy inhale and exhale. And then the words that he knew neither of them would ever forget.

"You die."

The voice was oddly sexless.

Kiera gasped and put a hand over her mouth. But it was too late.

Travis had no doubt that the caller had heard. He imagined their satisfaction at the fact that their victim was frightened. He was glad that for good measure his own phone was recording the call.

"You'll die before you'll ever testify. Die," the voice repeated.

The connection broke and the phone went dead.

"Damn it," Travis said and looked at Kiera.

She wasn't looking at him.

"Someone else is out there," she said in a whisper. "Someone else knows who I am, where I am. They never spoke before—the other calls, I mean. And that voice, it gave me chills."

He took her hands. They were limp, her palms damp. He looked into her eyes.

"They're words, Kiera. Nothing more. You're safe and I'll make sure you remain safe." Meanwhile, his mind was going through the options. Who this might be, what the level of threat might be. He needed to speak to James. They needed to discuss this development and analyze what he'd recorded.

"How do they have my number? How do they know I was a witness? Who squealed?"

She was hitting valid points. Points that had him concerned. There'd been leaks in the emergency system before—rare, but it had happened. While most were dedicated to their jobs and usually close-mouthed, there had been a few over the years who had revealed information that was never meant to go public. Had it happened again? And then, of course, there was the wild card. The bus driver who had initially rescued her had sworn no oath of secrecy. The chances that the time of her rescue had been leaked were high. That would explain these calls and justify the possibility that this was just a prankster who had also discovered her identity.

"There was someone else—the man in jail wasn't acting alone."

"Kiera," he began.

She stood up.

"It doesn't matter what I say, does it?" she said angrily. "You're not going to believe me. Despite the fact that I was there." The last words sounded defeated.

"I'm not saying that." He quelled the frustration from showing in his voice. She didn't need that. These phone calls on top of everything else were too much. He took a calming breath. "I'm not discounting what you're saying, Kiera. I can't deny that there's someone out there threatening your life. I heard them. It definitely needs to be looked into. But I don't want you worrying about your safety. No matter what the intent of these calls, no matter who it is, you're safe here. I'm going to ensure that."

She moved away from him and turned her back. She was looking out to the front lawn where the rising sun was dispersing the shadows. "I heard that voice before. The night when I was taken." Her voice dropped off.

He turned to stare at her. She was determined that she'd been the victim of two kidnappers. Maybe it was time to give the theory more consideration than anyone had up to this point. He knew that it didn't fit the profile that had been built in the year-long investigation and that was why the idea was getting pushback. But profiles were not written in stone.

There was a pensive and rather frightened look on her face. "One of my kidnappers had a very unusual voice. It sounded exactly like that," she said. "But I've already told you that. I don't know why I'm bothering to do it again."

She was speaking so softly that he had to strain to hear her.

"Don't stop, Kiera," he encouraged.

"That was the voice of the second killer. I know it."

He looked at her with more than a little interest. He nodded, urging her to continue.

"It was dark," she said in a low voice that was close to a whisper. "But it was clear that there were two voices. One voice was different from the other, as different as their touch. It wasn't the one who was arrested. There were two people there—two kidnappers."

"You're sure?" he asked.

"Yes, damn it!" she said, anger flaring in her voice. "But no one believes me. They might believe me—maybe," she said with drawled-out sarcasm. "When it's too late."

"It will never be too late," he said. "That's why I'm here and I've never failed in a case. I won't fail you now."

"You promise?" she asked with a touch of hope replacing the anger.

"I promise," he said.

"These calls will end tonight," he assured her. It was easier to take the emotion out of the equation by defaulting to work and business. It was the only way to dodge what was stirring in the room, or more aptly, within him. It was an attraction he couldn't seem to stop.

"Can I keep this?" he asked as he held her phone up. "I'll get you another, a prepaid," he said as he saw the look of doubt in her face. He wanted her cooperation but with or without it she wouldn't be handling these kinds of calls. From now on, he or someone else on the team would be accepting any further prank calls. She had enough to deal with.

Slowly she nodded. And he felt humble at the fact that in that one gesture she'd offered the last of her doubt, that she'd given him her trust.

She was pale and quiet. He worried for her, for her well-being. She'd survived a lot, more than most people ever survived in a lifetime. Had the call been too much, compounded with all the trauma she'd so recently escaped?

"I need to make a call. Will you be alright for a few minutes?"

"I'll be fine," she said.

He paused.

"Really," she assured him. "I'm fine."

Outside, he pulled his phone out of his pocket and hit one of the numbers in memory, the FBI's security team. Two minutes later he'd spoken with Serene Deveraux, their security expert. She was the head of that unit and had been for as long as he had been a marshal. He quickly had her assurance that she'd do everything possible to trace the call. Around him, the surrounding homes were beginning to come to life as they prepared to begin a day that, for them, was no different from any other.

His phone buzzed. It was Serene returning his call with news that only confirmed what he already knew.

"My guess is that whoever is making the call is using a burner," she said in her usual matter-of-fact, get-the-job-done voice.

The fact that they were using a prepaid phone didn't surprise him. It was what he'd suspected.

He shoved the phone in his pocket and went inside where he could smell coffee brewing and could see Kiera in the kitchen. She moved easily around the small area. And, as much as he'd tried to be objective and treat her like any other case, he had to admit that she wasn't any other case. Her in-your-face attitude on the lawn yesterday morning was an act of defiance that defined their first meeting, an act that had both surprised and intrigued him. She'd been kick-ass from the beginning and despite the reasons for his being here, he couldn't help the fact that he was attracted to her. He kept telling himself that it was nothing more than superficial. After all, she was rounded in all the right places. A full bottom that he'd love to…

Stop it, Johnson. He pushed the thought from his mind and immediately regretted it, for that thought was replaced by that of the creep who had almost had his way with her. The anger he felt at that thought was like nothing he'd felt before. For the first time in his life he wanted a man to die. For the first time—he wanted revenge.

Chapter Seven

Travis put the bowl down. It was one of a set that were cream colored and scalloped in blue, each with a different farm scene. He guessed that they were another of Kiera's craft-sale finds. He'd just whipped eggs, and the cheese, tomato, onion and assorted spices were ready to go. He'd been in the midst of making her an omelet for breakfast. It was six o'clock, an early start to the day. It had been a day with a rough start. Getting the third set of anonymous calls had been upsetting for Kiera and something he needed to follow up on with Serene and beef up security.

He glanced over his shoulder. Kiera was nursing her coffee with a hand on either side of the cup. She was looking gaunt, as if it had all been too much. And he wondered how it could not be. It took a special kind of person to bounce back from what she'd endured. He was going to make sure that she started the day out right. With something that stuck to her ribs, as his grandmother was fond of saying. It was from her and his mother that he'd learned the art of cooking.

"It seems like a never-ending nightmare," she said.

"It will end," he assured her.

"I hope so," she said. But her voice seemed dull, almost absent of emotion.

Damn, he thought. Despite how well she'd been doing, right now she didn't look fine at all. She was sitting like a pale statue at the table. Her mind was obviously somewhere else. He could only imagine that that place was the recent and very ugly past. Was she thinking about her ordeal or about the phone call and her belief that the killer wasn't acting alone? While he had yet to admit anything to her, his gut told him that there might be some validity to her theory. But instinct and gut feelings wouldn't convince the FBI on the matter. He flipped his thoughts.

"Can I get you some more coffee?" he asked.

She didn't answer.

"Kiera?"

He sat down beside her, pulling his chair close to hers. Had he overestimated her resiliency? If needed, he'd be willing to change the shift schedule more than he already had and stay with her through all of today, as well. She needed familiarity; she needed him. He didn't allow himself to consider that last thought.

There was something that spoke of desperation in the look she gave him. He squeezed her hands, too tightly.

"Ouch. It's okay, Travis."

"Sorry," he said but even as he let her hands go, he remained beside her. He'd be her support for as long as she needed him. But her eyes were dark, brooding, filled with memories that were deep and soul disturbing. He couldn't stop looking at her. He felt for her on a level that he couldn't quite quantify. It was as if everything about her mattered—to him.

The connection caught his breath and left him speechless. It was as if there were something special that bonded them in a way neither of them could fathom. He pushed the thoughts from his mind. Seconds slipped into a minute and then two.

"I'm lucky to be alive," she murmured. "And I want to live. But someone out there wants me dead."

He didn't dispute what she was saying. There was no disputing the reality of the threat.

His mind went back to the report. A transit driver, Sophia Antonia, had found her minutes before dawn. The driver's report stated that she'd seen a woman's silhouette under the glow of the streetlight. At the time, she'd thought she'd been seeing things. But as she got closer, she'd seen Kiera weaving at the entrance of the alley. She'd seemed fragile, broken even, but she'd waved her hands over her head in a plea for help. At first, Sophia thought she was drunk or high. She said the torn medical scrubs and tunic made her realize that something was very wrong.

He marveled at how luck had both saved Kiera's life and almost taken it. She had been lucky that Sophia had been there that morning. It was a rough area of town and not the bus driver's usual route to work. But she was much earlier than usual. As a result, she'd taken the unusual route to grab a cup of coffee at a place that catered to truckers and was open at that hour of the morning.

Sophia had been blocks from her destination when she'd seen the woman stagger from the alley into the light of a nearby streetlight. At first, she hadn't intended to stop. The fact that she'd backtracked was amazing in itself. It wasn't a place or time where most would have stopped to help an unknown woman. But Sophia had claimed some instinct told her that Kiera was different, that she desperately needed help. Then, as she'd turned her car around and the headlights had shone on Kiera, she'd seen the state she was in and known then that there was something very wrong. She knew despite the time and place, she had to stop. It wasn't total bravery; Sophia admitted that she wasn't unarmed. She went nowhere without her inherited Colt Special. And with that in her hand and her phone in her back pocket, she'd gotten out of her vehicle to investigate. As she'd approached, she claimed that Kiera had stood there unmoving with her torn tunic and pants flapping in the breeze.

Then Kiera had spoken the only words she was to speak until she arrived in the hospital.

Help me.

And the transit driver had.

She'd taken Kiera to her vehicle, put her in the backseat, then called 911 and waited for help to arrive. The state Kiera was in had the woman nervous as to who might have done this to her. And she'd admitted to locking the doors and sitting poised at the wheel, with the engine running, ready to take off if necessary.

"I'm fine, Travis. It's just…" She brought his attention back to where it needed to be, on her.

"You're sure?" he asked, taking her hands in his and squeezing them.

"Positive," she said with a smile and pulled her hands free. "Hungry," she said with a tentative smile. "What's the time on that omelet?"

TEN MINUTES LATER she took the last bite and pushed the plate to the side.

"This is the best omelet I've ever tasted," she said. "You're a fantastic cook. Thank you." She stood up, picking up her plate and reaching over to pick up his. "Where'd you learn to cook like that?"

"My grandmother insisted I learn," he said with a smile as he put his hand over hers. "And my mother," he finished. "Let me clean up."

"No," she replied. "I need something to do and you said you had to go into the office."

"You're sure?" He didn't feel concern at leaving her alone. She wasn't a runner. That he was sure of and that was what the FBI had been concerned about. He knew that for the most part, James trusted his assessment. He'd make sure she was safe and he wouldn't be gone long. But, in that time, he'd arranged for the area to be patrolled by a police officer and later this afternoon Devon would take over. In the meantime, he had no qualms about her safety. He'd covered all the angles.

"Positive," she said. "I need to get back to a routine. Nothing better than dishes to take one's mind off things."

"Alright," he said, appreciating the way she was able to return to normal despite the trauma she'd been through. He guessed much of it was pretend on her part. And, while it wasn't healthy in the long run, in the short term it helped her cope. "I won't be gone long. An hour tops. You know my number—call me if there's any trouble, anything at all," he said. "I'll get a patrol car in the area while I'm gone." For she might not be a runner but he wasn't one hundred percent confident, considering her belief and the calls, about her safety.

"I'll be alright."

"Keep the doors locked," he said a few minutes later with his hand on the doorknob. "Call me…" he repeated.

"No worries," she said.

And she stood on the step as he pulled away, a lone figure who looked too small, too vulnerable. The memory of her standing there, of her vulnerability, stuck in his mind. As a result, he drove a little too fast, trying to shorten the time he was gone, the time she might be alone.

Chapter Eight

"I need electronic security in place and I need it yesterday," Travis said. He was in the FBI office in Cheyenne. He and Serene had already gone through a minute's worth of niceties. He didn't have any more time than that.

"I'm sorry to rush this but…"

"No problem," Serene interrupted. "Keep the facts coming—you know I don't do well with small talk."

Despite being head of her unit, Serena was still very hands-on. He knew that other than giving her the specs of Kiera's property, she'd handle the rest without his help.

Serene made a note of all the relevant details, asking him pertinent questions as she typed. "I'll have a man out within the hour," she said and looked up from her computer screen. "Motion detectors, cameras, the works. There won't be anything that happens around her place that we won't be on top of."

"Today?"

"Today," she promised. "Give your witness the

heads-up that there'll be activity around the house. Better yet, make sure you're there."

If he didn't know her as well as he did, he would think that she was implying that he needed to be told how to do his job. But he knew that Serene didn't mean to undermine. That was just her manner. He'd known her for years and had a friendship that had begun with a series of misguided dates.

"Sit and we'll finish this up," she said without looking at him.

He pulled out a chair. They both knew the drill. He provided the information she needed and offered photos of the problem areas he'd identified. He listed the specifics almost by rote as he'd memorized them yesterday when he'd first seen the place.

"The system will be in place by early afternoon," she said as she looked up from her computer screen. Her eyes were molten and dark and, right now, razor-sharp.

"I'll set up a system that will be monitored from here. But you'll also be able to access it. I've made it inaccessible inside the unit based on what you've said of your witness."

"I can work with that," Travis said.

She looked at him. "There's something else. The phone. What are you going to do about that?"

"I bought a prepaid for her to use and I took hers. That way if there're any more of those calls she won't be receiving them." He put the phone on the desk. He'd been clear with Kiera that her family and friends wouldn't be able to contact her, but that she could still reach them. She'd promised him that she'd limit her calls and not reveal any vital information like her current situation with law enforcement or anything regarding the case, including the threatening calls. She'd agreed and said that she'd warn her friends that she'd be out of communication for a time.

He'd been surprised that it wasn't an issue for her and more surprised when he learned that she had no close family. In fact, he'd not only been surprised but floored. He knew that she had been orphaned. He knew that she'd been raised by an aunt and he knew what the file had said, but he hadn't taken that information literally. In the back of his mind he'd always thought that there was someone.

He couldn't imagine being alone like that. He couldn't imagine not having to make sure there was some way to communicate with people who had always been there for you. In his vibrant and close-knit family, that wouldn't happen. His family had deep roots in Cheyenne although some of them had since scattered farther afield. But none of them would be okay with being out of touch with him. In fact, they'd proven their need to stay in touch over the years—and when he could be, he was there for them, always leaving a way for them to be in contact. Only last week, he'd stopped by his aunt's apartment to help her move a dresser, and minutes ago he'd made a quick call to check on his mother, as his father was on a business trip. The fact that Kiera had no biological family was something he couldn't comprehend. But she claimed her family were her friends, even her coworkers. And she'd been concerned about them and relieved when he'd told her that she could call them using her pre-paid. The phone's number would be blocked. She'd already been instructed not to give the phone num-ber out. He wasn't ready to trust anyone, not even her inner circle.

"Excellent," Serene said bringing him out of his thoughts of Kiera. "We'll monitor the calls. I'll try to run a trace on anything suspicious. Give me the number of the prepaid and I'll forward anything per-sonal directly to her."

"That's it," he said a minute later as he stood up. "Anything else and I'll be in touch."

With the surveillance issue in motion, he headed down the hall.

You'll die before you'll ever testify.

The words were dire. They were not words that could or should be ignored. Crank call or not, he couldn't assume that it was benign. His gut was tell-ing him that there was weight behind the threat, that it might not be chance that had her receiving those calls. That was why he was here.

His steps echoed as he strode down the hallway. A minute later he was outside James's office.

He gave one hard knock on the door. The sound echoed down the corridor. He didn't knock twice. James was expecting him. His hand was on the door-knob when he heard the greeting and was told to come inside.

"What's going on, Trav?" James asked after Travis

had taken a seat. "I heard you're lining up electronic security on the witness's home."

"I did. Kiera's been receiving anonymous phone calls since she returned home." He went into the details of the calls.

"Have you witnessed any of these calls?" James interrupted.

Travis was not fazed by the interruption. He would have been more disturbed if James hadn't interrupted. For that was his habit. He was an interactive, if slightly abrasive, listener. The only time that fact changed was if the topic had no interest or relevance for him.

"Not until early this morning. The last call was five after five. For the first time there was a voice." He paused. "She's adamant that there were two perps that night."

James was looking at him with interest.

"Serene has determined that the calls were made on burners."

"So, there's no way of linking them to a person, an account," James said thoughtfully.

"No. And they appear to have been made from various points throughout the city."

He looked over James's shoulder where he could see a partial view of Cheyenne's skyline. Cheyenne was a small city. It wasn't a place where one expected a woman to be afraid for her life. But crime occurred everywhere, even where it was least expected. If nothing else, his career had taught him that.

James sat back with a look of concern on his face.

He laced his fingers and batted his thumbs. "Initially, our biggest threat was the chance of the witness disappearing. Running if she felt threatened. This will only exacerbate the potential for that problem."

Travis didn't say anything to that. The possibility that the witness would run had been a concern for the feds since the beginning. They based that fear on the fact that their witness was insistent on her belief that there was more than one perpetrator. Another threat could cause her risk of flight to increase. He wasn't so sure that they were right. After meeting Kiera, after seeing how much she cared for her condo, how much she cared for the cat she'd adopted and how much she loved her life and job—he saw no risk of flight.

"I don't think running is a problem. I think we have a different situation to be concerned about," he said. "The last call threatened her with death."

"Did the others?" James asked without skipping a beat at the switch in direction the conversation was taking.

"She says no. According to her, no one spoke during the other calls. The first of the set was only a hang-up and the second was heavy breathing. Like I said, according to Kiera, always at the same time, same duration. Until this morning when the last call changed everything."

"This has been going on for three mornings, if we include today. And she didn't feel that it might have been important to notify us immediately?"

"She mentioned the calls to the police officer on duty, the first morning they happened. But she said that, despite how distraught she was over them, he'd basically blown her off. Told her she was imagining things as a result of the trauma she'd been through."

"So not only did he push aside a key piece of evidence, he decided to play amateur psychologist." James swore, as he turned his attention to his computer. "I'll be looking into this. In a case like this something like that should not have been ignored." He frowned. "I'll be pulling him off this case, that's for sure."

His fingers flew on the keys as if making notes as he talked. Seconds passed and he stopped, pushed the computer to the side.

"So, tell me more about these phone calls."

"According to her, nothing was said, just some heavy breathing, that was it. This morning, I was at her door at five and missed the first phone call. She said they hung up after she answered. Except, they're at exactly the same time. Five minutes to five and five minutes after."

"I wish I felt comfortable saying that it was just another loon out there," James said. "Or, even that it was someone jumping on local news to get their jollies. But that seems unlikely. We've kept the information on this case pretty bare-bones, at least what the public is hearing. And the most disturbing aspect is the time that last call is coming in. The same time as her rescue." He shook his head. "That time was never released."

Travis looked at James and neither of them said

anything for a minute. Then James leaned back. "Five after five was the time the emergency call came in."

Travis nodded.

"A leak? Possible. Unfortunately, it's happened before." He pushed back in his chair and looked at Travis. "So, these calls have been going on since she got home?"

"That's pretty much it," Travis said. "The last three mornings. This morning she claimed the first call came in as it always did. No one was there when she answered. I heard the second at five minutes after five exactly the time she claims that the last of each of the previous sets occurred."

James leaned forward, a frown on his face and a look of expectation in his eyes.

"I put it on speaker phone and the voice I heard was androgynous. It had no inflection, can't even verify if it was human or machine-made. What I can tell you was that the caller threatened her life. Here," he pulled out his phone. "I'll play it."

When it was over, James again pushed back his chair, this time with enough force to go back a few feet. His arms were behind his head and a frown was on his face.

"Damn," James said. "I know you've stated that she isn't giving signs of running but this could just tip things. What she experienced was unimaginable and now this."

"It's not good," Travis agreed.

"That was all there was?"

Travis nodded. "Too short to trace. But she claims

that the voice she heard sounds like the voice of a second person involved in the kidnapping."

"Yet we only made one arrest. Only one killer was in our sights until this." James ran a hand through the pouf of curly black hair that centered just above the classic buzz cut on the sides of his head. "I don't like the sound of this. We can't afford to ignore it. Of course, if you have no trace, we have nothing to go on."

"I've given Kiera's phone to Serene to monitor and given Kiera a prepaid. She's setting up surveillance."

James didn't acknowledge the phone transfer but instead said, "Good call on the surveillance."

Travis said nothing. What he'd done was only another detail like all the others—part of his job. He changed the subject.

"She's different than I expected even from your initial report," he said, determined to address some of the key components of this assignment.

"What do you mean different?" James asked.

"She's more grounded than you think. I don't see a flight risk at all. In fact, I'd say just the opposite. She's determined that justice is served. But these phone calls…" He shook his head. "A death threat isn't something to discount. Could there be a leak? Did someone talk about what happened, mention the time that she was found?"

"I hope to hell not," James said. "I trust my team."

"There's the hospital, the emergency crew, a string of people involved. It only takes one of them to open their mouth."

"I'll put someone on it. Heads will be rolling if that's the case."

"And she might be right. Maybe this is a perp that's flown under the wire."

"A second kidnapper." James shook his head. "One thing I've learned in this job is never say never."

He stood up. "Whatever the motivation for the calls, we can't ignore this. Keep our witness safe and keep me up to date. In the meantime." He looked at his watch. "I've got another case breathing up my tail. I'll have to trust you on this one as I always do." He said the last with a laugh.

Travis didn't ask what else James had on his plate. He didn't need to know. He had one mission and one mission only, and that was keeping Kiera not only alive, but safe. He wouldn't jeopardize either one of those mandates for details not related to her and her case.

Chapter Nine

Arranging surveillance, meeting with James—all of it had taken longer than Travis had expected. It was early afternoon by the time he returned to Kiera's condo. Serene had promised the security would be in place by the end of the afternoon. In the meantime, he needed to update Kiera on all that had happened.

Her front door opened before he'd reached the end of the sidewalk. Kiera stood with one hand on the door and the other on the jamb. She smiled, and he felt a welcome like he had come home. He shook the feeling off.

"How'd it go?" she asked as she ushered him inside and closed the door.

The unease and troubled demeanor that had radiated off her this morning was gone. Now there was an aura about her that he found calming. That surprised him considering all she'd been through. But there was so much about her that was a surprise. She wasn't fitting the profile her file had painted. He couldn't pigeonhole her and he found that refreshing.

"The feds have agreed to electronic surveillance.

Your condo and the area around it will be monitored twenty-four-seven," Travis said. He regretted what he'd said, how he'd said it, when he saw the look on her face. He regretted that he hadn't alerted her to his intentions before he left. But, for him, this type of procedure was standard. He'd forgotten, that for her, it wasn't.

"Is that necessary?"

"Better safe than sorry," he replied. "The anonymous phone calls are likely nothing more than someone with a sick sense of humor. But we'll have an eye on your place just to make sure." She'd already said that she believed the voice sounded like the second kidnapper. Repeating that fact now wouldn't move the case forward but it would more than likely upset her. Upset was not what he wanted their star witness to be so, for now, he downplayed.

"You mean close my bedroom door when I'm changing?" she asked with a slight smile.

It took him a minute to react. He hadn't expected a joke. In fact, it hit him so sideways that he didn't react at all.

"Kidding," she said before he could answer.

She went to the fridge and opened it, bringing out two bottles of water.

"Here," she said. "I imagine you haven't had a break or a drink since you left."

"Your instincts are spot on," he said with a laugh and she offered him an answering smile as she sat down on the couch.

He took the drink she offered. Flavored water, lemon, something they admitted they both liked.

"Thank you," he said as he chugged back a couple of generous swallows before recapping it. He sat down on the couch beside her.

"As you already know, I won't be here every day," he said. "There'll be other marshals taking shifts." He looked at his watch. "Devon Gowan is due in half an hour. He'll be taking the next shift." The shifts were long but not as long as the time he'd spent. He'd stayed until he knew things were stable and Kiera felt safe. "But if you need me, call—I'll more than likely be in the vicinity."

"I could have guessed that."

This time the smile she gave him was rather quirky and her eyes had a look. It was like she knew everything about him.

"Really?"

"You're not that hard to read, Travis," she said. "You don't give up control easily and you feel responsible for me. Although you shouldn't. Despite what's happened I have been taking care of myself for a long time."

"I know," he said feeling slightly chastised. "Reece Blackburn will take the shift after Devon. Just so you know who's who."

"I'll be fine, really," she said. "I have everything I need including the update you gave me on the men who will replace you—Devon and then Reece. You're a worrier, aren't you?" she asked with a smile.

He was glad to hear the light, almost teasing tone

in her voice. She'd been weighted down with enough darkness. Unfortunately, until this trial was over, it was a darkness that was a long way from ending. She'd been through hell. He imagined that a trauma like she'd been through was forever burned in one's memory, an inescapable nightmare. She'd literally escaped both rape and death. For her to tease, to see humor in anything now, so soon after was, he hoped, a promising sign.

"You worry too much, Trav."

The diminutive of his name stuck in his mind. Only those closest to him ever called him that. He wondered what that meant in the scope of their relationship. Did she feel the connection he felt? He pushed the thoughts away. There was no relationship, not like that—not ever.

"Is there something else?" she asked.

"No," he said. "There's been nothing more. But we aren't taking any chances with your safety. Last night's threat was enough. I want you to stay inside. Like I said, we'll have a marshal on the grounds most of the time and video surveillance twenty-four-seven. Any sign of a problem and someone will be at your door in minutes."

The smile was gone. Her face was pale.

It was his fault for reminding her of the drama that was currently her life. "I'm sorry…"

"No." She shook her head. "Thank you. I appreciate all of this."

"Remember, you're safe. Help is one phone call away. I or someone else will be continually cruising the area. We have surveillance in place—there's no chance of anyone getting to you. Plus, the serial killer who began all this is locked up. He can't get to you."

"He can't," she said, her green eyes shining with determination as they focused on him. "There's more than one. There's..." she said.

She could be right. As he'd admitted to James, he was beginning to believe there had to be something to it.

"I know, there's nothing to prove what the crazy woman claims," she said with a hint of resentment in her voice. "You're wrong. I can't give you details but I know there was another person. It's not just my imagination."

He'd tried not to frown, to keep his face placid. And yet, some of what she said was right. This case wasn't over because the killer went to jail; there was something else, something they'd all missed.

"I heard both of them the night they took me," she persisted.

"I know what you think, about there being two serial killers, a partnership. It's rare but I haven't discounted it. In fact, I spoke to my superior about it."

She leaned back against the wall, as if standing without support was too much.

"If there's someone else out there, we'll catch them, I promise."

She nodded, her lips tense. But a look of gratitude was in her eyes as she took a step toward him.

"Thank you," she said. "For believing."

She touched his arm and the heat of her touch seemed to sear his skin.

"I appreciate everything you've done but I've at least had a few hours' sleep. You need to rest," she said. Her eyes seemed to take in everything about him. "We've been joined at the hip for the last thirty-two hours," she continued. "And spending the night in your vehicle was no way to get a good night's rest. You can't be watching me almost twenty-four-seven. And," she interrupted when he was about to state his argument to her accurate observation. "I know you haven't been here all the time. And you don't need to be. No one does. It's enough to know that you're a phone call away and that there will soon be a monitoring system. Having someone here the majority of the time is more than enough. Being watched by someone in your office, well, I couldn't be safer." She lifted her hand from his arm, but the heat didn't dissipate; she was still too close.

His phone dinged. It was a text message from Devon.

She stood up and went to the window, looking out.

"Devon will be here in a few minutes," he said to Kiera as he joined her.

"Good," she said with a smile. "You'll be able to get some sleep."

She turned and gave him a gentle push toward the door.

"Hey," he said with a playful tone to his voice.

"Get going," she said with a smile.

"Determined, are you?" he flirted. *Damn it, man, cool it*, he chastised himself.

"Always," she replied with a serious tone.

He knew that she'd been running her own life too long to play by other's rules. It was a trait he'd picked up on immediately after reading her file. It was there that he'd read of her guardian's death. It was there that he'd learned how she'd been independent since the age of eighteen. It impressed him even now to know that she'd put herself through a master's degree in nursing while never losing sight of her goal. She'd worked toward her chosen career while holding a part-time job and living alone.

At the door, he turned to face her.

"You haven't had much sleep yourself," he said.

He was leaving her safety in the hands of another man. Despite the fact that Devon was a friend, it didn't sit well. He didn't want to think of all the reasons why that might be the case. He couldn't go there, for to go there—to where his feelings lay—would break the barriers he was attempting to build.

"I'm fine," she said as if she could read his mind. "Quit worrying. A bath and a nap are all I need."

"Keep your door locked. Devon will be around. He may check in from time to time but if that becomes bothersome, just tell him."

She gave him a smile that didn't quite reach her eyes this time.

"Thanks, Travis. All of this makes me feel better, especially after last night."

"We'll keep you safe. You have my number…"

"I have my gun too," she reminded him as she'd done earlier.

He said nothing. He didn't need to be reminded of that. She had a Colt .45 in her possession. She also had no training, no practice with firearms that he knew of. A gun in the hands of someone not used to firing it could be deadlier than someone who was unarmed. The weapon could be used against her. He could only hope that that situation didn't occur. Instead he skated over the comment. He'd instructed Devon to notify him if anything changed, even a feeling of an imminent change—anything at all. He wanted to know. In the meantime, she'd be all right. She had to be.

"By the way," she said, interrupting his thoughts. "Your security installation expert—I believe that's what he called himself—he called me from the driveway before ever getting out of his vehicle. I'm not sure what he expected to find here, a fire-breathing dragon? What the heck did you say to him?"

Travis chuckled. "I didn't say anything. At least nothing that wasn't true." He'd warned Jed that she was jumpy as a result of all that had happened and she also had a weapon. Jed had obviously taken the necessary precautions not to surprise her.

A knock on the door interrupted his rather drawn-out goodbye. His hand was on the doorknob. He wasn't ready to hand her safety over to anyone else completley, even someone as skilled as Devon. But no one was at their peak with no sleep and if he were honest he'd admit that he'd reached his limit. He was done. He was only human, and he needed sleep. He opened the door.

"Looking a little worn, pal," Devon Gowan said as he entered the condo. "Age getting to you?"

"Thanks," Travis said with a grin. Devon had been part of the group that had gone out for drinks to celebrate Travis's thirtieth birthday. At the jokes about old age and turning thirty, Devon had only laughed as he'd reached his thirty-fifth over six months ago. Thirty, he'd joked, was a nothing birthday.

Devon held out his hand to Kiera. "Devon. Good to meet you."

Kiera took it without hesitation. "I'm glad you're here."

She nodded toward Travis.

"He needs a break."

Travis couldn't help but smile. There was a maternal note to her voice that he hadn't heard before. He was feeling slightly better about leaving her.

"Thought I'd at least introduce myself and after that I'll make myself scarce," Devon said. "I won't get in your way. All I ask is that you remain on your property. And if for any reason you plan to leave—I need to know. Although I'd prefer…"

"That I stay here."

"Yes, ma'am." He gave her a nod. "Here's my number if you need to call."

He and Travis exchanged some final details and a minute later the door closed behind Devon.

Kiera looked at him with doubt in her eyes.

"He's good," Travis assured her.

"He's not you," she said.

He wasn't sure what she meant by that and he wasn't going to put any meaning into it. He couldn't. She was an assignment, nothing more. Still, he hesitated. If leaving had been difficult before, it was worse now. She was more than an assignment. Although even admitting it to himself felt wrong. He needed to put a stop to his feelings.

"Go," she said and gave him a light push. "Get some sleep. I'll be fine."

He hoped she was right as he closed the door behind him.

RAGE RAN WHITE HOT through every pore.

Eric should be here and he wasn't because of that cursed nurse. Because of their last victim. The nurse thought she'd gotten away. She was wrong. Her rotten scent could be sniffed out; she'd be found. For one, her name was on her tag and even though Eric had panicked and thrown her purse into a Dumpster, it hadn't been hard to find where she lived. For the first time since they'd begun the spree, they'd stayed near the city where their last victim was taken. In every other kill, they'd been hundreds of miles away before the body got cold. Now there was no leaving, not until the work was done, not until Kiera Connell was dead.

The pen snapped, and a drop of red ink hit one hand and landed on the edge of her freshly pressed T-shirt. The red stain looked like blood. And it was a reminder that blood was life and the ability to take life was power.

She'd planned to go back to Denver. There they could set up house together—rest, have a stay-cation before they hit the road again. That had been her plan all along. Once they'd finished with the latest victim, they'd retire for a while. Whether it was a month or two, or even a year, she didn't know. But the plan had been solid, she'd already made steps in that direction. That had all been before Eric had fallen into the hands of the law.

Anger raced through her. For now, all that was ruined. They'd left the victim restrained and cruised the city, dragging out the moment when they could enjoy their captive. It's what they always did—the best was saved for last: rape and murder. It was like holding off opening a Christmas present. At least that's how she's explained it to Eric when she'd first begun the ritual. This time, she'd agreed to grab them something to eat and dropped Eric off. She knew that he'd wait for her. For he never raped unless she was there to watch. But the bitch had somehow escaped either in the time they'd cruised around together anticipating the final moments with her or while she'd been getting takeout and Eric had gone to the nearest convenience store for the cigarettes he refused to give up. He'd been back first and had obviously missed signs that the law's trap lay in wait. She'd been just behind him, far enough back to get away. Now, all that was left was revenge.

Kiera Connell had stolen the only person who mattered. And the phone calls had done nothing to release the anger. None of them, not even the rage and threat spewed on the last call. Kiera had ruined everything. Kiera needed to die, long and slow and painfully.

In the meantime, patience was all that was left.

But nothing came easy, nothing ever had. Even Eric had taken years to find. First there'd been enduring a marriage to someone who had put food on the table and grief in their bed. Years of abuse had ended in a brutal, messy way. A hammer in mid rant had ended it all. The burial spot would never be found. *Gone and run off* was as good an excuse as any when people asked, but few did. Now that was all in the past. The new life, the new name—all of it was the start of a life that had once been only a dream.

There'd been lonely years in between but it was then that the skills of the craft were honed. First on transients found along secondary highways, at least in the days before Eric.

Eric.

They'd had years of bliss. But, now it was over, he was gone and only anger was left.

Eric.

He'd been a teenage runaway, eager to learn— to be molded into the man he had become. Despite her rough marriage, she hadn't been that old herself. She'd been twenty-eight to his sixteen when she'd found him. He'd already spent a few years on the street. It was perfect. She was old enough to know more than he but young enough to understand him. And for years their sadistic crime spree had flown under the radar. But, as their crimes became more ambitious and the missing women began to add up, their actions gained notoriety. For the last year, people had lived in fear of them. It had been a wonderful time, a glorious time. The highs they'd felt during those exhilarating months as they'd crisscrossed the country were now only memories. The highs needed to come back but alone it was impossible. There was only one thing to do. While it wouldn't fix everything, it would give some satisfaction.

Justice.

To get justice, the last victim, the traitor, needed to die.

The authorities thought they could protect their star witness. They thought she was safe with Eric behind bars. They believed that Eric had run a one-man show.

What a laugh.

He didn't have it in him to have enjoyed and killed as many women as they had. On his own he was messy and far from able to plan and maneuver into the future. Alone, he would have been caught a long time ago.

The window of the van that had been home for the last three weeks needed to be washed. The van replaced the vehicle before, and the one before that. The vehicles had been temporary homes stolen from neglected and troubled places where the odds of their loss being reported was minimal to none. It was chilly. Was Eric cold? It was hard to stop worrying about someone who had been your responsibility for so many years. It was impossible to stop thinking of him now for he'd been everything, son—partner in crime.

This must finish on their terms, for Eric. Justice for Eric. It was the one thing that needed to be done. It was the only thing that would make everything right. The kill that was the most important and the one that would be the last. And whether it was or not, the excitement at the thought was like no other.

Chapter Ten

Early the next day, Travis knew one fact—sleep was
pointless. As much as he needed sleep, as much as
he had promised Kiera that he'd get some, he'd only
managed a few hours. He wouldn't have gotten even
that much if, for the last half day, James hadn't been
tied up with another case. But James would be in
his office now and while he could call, in a situation like this he always found face-to-face to be better. Fifteen minutes later he found himself again in
James's office.

"Grab a coffee and have a seat," James said. "I
can only imagine that you've had some long nights."

"That goes without saying," he said. He poured a
cup of coffee out of the carafe that was always at the
ready in James's office. He put the carafe down and
pulled out a chair that sat at an angle from James's
desk. He was anxious to see what, if anything, was
new. He hoped that there was a lead on the anonymous phone calls.

"Exactly as you thought, Travis. Serene confirmed
that they're using prepaid phones. There's no way of

tracking who made the calls," James said. "What we do know is that whoever made them did it from a variety of locations within the city. They were all made from the edges of downtown."

Within the city.

"Someone could have Kiera's ID in their hands. Her bag was never found," Travis said. His gut screamed that these calls were connected but…

"If we didn't have the perpetrator behind bars, that would be a troubling fact," James said. "Or, if I believed at all that there was a second perp still on the loose. I've looked at the evidence and I can't go there, Trav." He pushed away from the desk and leaned back in his chair. "Unfortunately, the wrong person picked up her ID and decided to play games with her rather than return it. And now they've made a sadistic game of it. A crime in itself but not the crime you think."

"I see where you're coming from, but I think it's more than that, James. I've got a bad feeling. And Kiera is still convinced that there's more than one killer."

"Convince me," James said as he locked his hands behind his head. "We have the killer behind bars and there've been no killings since he's been incarcerated. Never mind the fact that the evidence indicated he was acting alone. But it's becoming increasingly clear that these calls are not something we can discount. What the hell are they? What's the connection? I'm just not getting this."

"I agree. They're serious," Travis said. "I've gone through the history over and over. After her discharge from the hospital she becomes the victim of telephone harassment. And that harassment has carried on for three nights, or to be exact, three pre-dawn calls, the second call always occurring at exactly the same time that the original 911 call came in. And then the last call is a threat on her life." He smacked a hand on James's desk. "Damn it. I don't know what the connection is, if any. All of it is too coincidental. And none of it can be overlooked. A threat on her life. She needs more protection than we're giving her."

"I agree." James pushed his chair back from his desk, his hands interlocked behind his head.

"Is it possible that there is something that we're missing?"

James shook his head. "I don't know, Travis. I know that using a prepaid phone was more than likely the work of someone who didn't want to get caught. I agree with you there. It definitely involved planning. But planning for what?" He turned to the window as if the answer would lie there. "I can't imagine there could be a connection. It seems like too much of a long shot. And a second serial killer—other than the witness claiming that she heard someone else—there's no evidence at all to take us in that direction. A yearlong investigation turned up no evidence that there was anything more than the one man, Eric Solomon."

Travis stood up. He was frustrated at not having an answer, at not being able to solve this, to give it all a proper fix that would make Kiera perfectly safe. To do that, he needed answers. "I know two serial killers is a long shot. I agree with you there. But these calls, whoever and whatever they are, have to end."

"So, we've reached an agreement. The protection will be upped. Make the protection twenty-four-seven. From here on in, your team is on-site. We can't take the risk. Until we've figured out what the hell is going on, we play it safe."

Five minutes later, Travis left James's office. He was somewhat satisfied but still troubled. The evidence they had was heading in a direction that he didn't like. It was the same direction, the same theory, that Kiera believed and which, until now, he'd discounted. That had all spun on its head. Now her claim of two killers seemed even less of an impossibility. And, while James had yet to agree to such a theory, they were much closer to all being on the same page. Much closer than they had been yesterday.

He headed to the cafeteria where he grabbed a tray and a roast beef sandwich. Just before the till, he took an iced tea from the cooler, paid and found himself a seat in the far corner where he wouldn't be disturbed. He unwrapped the sandwich and started to eat, but his mind was elsewhere. He was thinking of everything that had transpired and brought them to this point. It was time to get his crew on board. The other marshals needed to know that the parameters of the assignment had changed. With Kiera's insistence that there was a second perpetrator and the reality of the phone calls, they had to tighten security. They'd thought the perpetrator was behind bars and that she was safe. If there was a second killer, she could be in danger. As a result, there would be no more being out of sight of the property for even a lunch break. He guessed they'd agree once they heard the circumstances, not that they had a choice.

He opened the app that allowed him to see the view from the cameras on Kiera's property. He panned the area at the front of the house. The grounds were quiet. He moved to the camera on the other side of her property and his finger froze before he could flip to another screen. For what he saw was the back of someone at the corner of her unit. There was no disputing that someone appeared to be casing her condo. It clearly wasn't Devon. Whoever it was, they were considerably shorter than that and Devon would have no reason to wear a hoodie or skulk around the property in such a manner. This was a stranger—someone who shouldn't be on the property, a trespasser. A moment later, the person was gone.

He swore and dropped the remains of his sandwich into the wrapper.

He was too far away. He punched Devon's number and waited. One ring, two. His fingers drummed on the table. A young man looked over at him. He recognized him as a new hire that James had mentioned. He was of no relevance. He was still training, an agent who was working with Serene at the moment. He looked through him, even as the guy watched him. He looked away. He had no time to worry about other people's curiosity. The phone continued to ring. Three rings and then four. Devon needed to get on this like yesterday except Devon wasn't answering. He hadn't ended the call before he was up and heading out the door.

He burst outside and within seconds was in the parking lot.

He bit off an expletive as he ran for his SUV and his mind checked off all the possibilities. He punched Devon's number again. Devon might have missed the call for a valid reason—a call to nature, who knew? Devon was his best hope to deal with the trespasser. But, as before, the phone rang unanswered before hitting voice mail.

Another curse flew. Where the hell was he and why wasn't he answering his phone? He'd have a word or two with him when this was over. His mind ran through the possibilities. He thought of calling Kiera, of warning her, and remembered her penchant for taking care of herself. She'd be more likely to want to face the trespasser with her gun. That could place her in worse danger than she might be in already. He had to get there before the unthinkable happened.

He was behind the wheel and had the SUV in gear almost in one motion. He was off with a screech of tires, driving as fast as he dared. Too fast, and without the warning sirens of an emergency vehicle, he'd endanger more lives than he was trying to save. He wanted to gun the engine and instead he had to slow down as he spotted kids playing. They were dangerously close to the street. He was in a residential area, no place for speeding. He had one eye on the children as he watched the speedometer and kept moving. He'd considered calling the police but even a few minutes ago, they'd have gotten there no sooner than he would, and the last thing he wanted was the chaos of multiple responders. All that aside, he had to get there. And he had to get there soon.

Kiera's life was at stake.

KIERA FELT LIKE she was trapped in her condo and had been for days. Yet it had been only five days since she'd been discharged from the hospital and a week before that since this whole horrid ordeal began and her life turned upside down. Wednesday, middle of the week, a day she often found herself scheduled at work. Work—a lifetime ago.

Since her discharge from the hospital, she hadn't gone farther than her own front yard. She was almost a prisoner in the house she loved so much. Travis popping in from time to time had made the confinement tolerable, even pleasant up until yesterday. But today staying another minute inside her condo felt unbearable. Without Travis's casual conversation, interspersed with shop talk she'd have been bored out of her mind. But having him there had livened up the day and made her feel less confined. Even his delving into more details of the horror that her life had become and the event that had changed her normal, even with that he'd kept her on edge in different ways, for she didn't know how she felt about him. He both entertained and interested her. The spark of attraction, of course, had helped and the time had flown by. But all that had changed since he'd left. Devon remained outside and, while he was a nice man, he didn't excite her the way Travis had. She guessed it worked both ways and maybe that's why Devon kept to himself. He'd check in every few hours and then only for a minute or less. That wasn't the same. She missed Travis.

Travis.

She couldn't help thinking of him. He was like no man she'd met before. She wished she'd met him under different circumstances, that might have changed everything. Maybe they could date like normal human beings. But she was normal no longer. She was a victim of crime. She was a witness. She'd been in the company of an evil that she didn't want to imagine, never mind think of. She wanted to forget that it had happened, but she couldn't. For she'd never escaped, not really. The danger had followed her. She knew it. She sensed it.

She shivered. Something felt different. She felt alone—vulnerable.

Devon had left on an errand and to grab an early lunch. He'd popped his head in to tell her that and she'd invited him to share lunch with her. If nothing else, she could use the company. But he was adamant about not imposing on her in any way. At the time, she hadn't disagreed even though she could have used the company.

While she was not privy to his thoughts, it seemed he wanted to reassure her. And he had reminded her that he'd be only a phone call away. Except, he'd left his phone behind. It was all because she'd asked for a minute of his time before he left. It was then that he'd dropped his phone. She'd found it beside the garbage after his car had pulled away. She thought it might have slipped out of his pocket when he was moving one of the boxes of recyclables.

Since then she'd heard it ring a few times but left it. Who was calling Devon and why was none of her business. She heard the phone ring again and turned away from it.

She had to get out. She felt trapped, like the walls were closing in. She needed fresh air. Despite her earlier thoughts and unease, she'd never felt anything but safe in this neighborhood. She didn't think any of that had changed. She hadn't jogged in almost two weeks and she missed it. She wouldn't venture farther than her block. She'd just do a repetitive circuit of the block until she ran off some steam. In her bedroom, she changed into a worn tank top and shorts.

She guessed that Travis wouldn't like this idea either. But there had been no physical danger since she'd returned home, and one thing she'd learned about him was that he could be overcautious. So, while she wouldn't be talked out of this, she would follow the rules. With Devon gone, she'd let the FBI know what she was doing. She put in a call at the number at FBI headquarters that was for any updates or problems with surveillance. The woman she talked to was insistent that she not do this. Kiera didn't give the argument much space. She wasn't asking permission, only giving a courtesy notification. She hung up before the woman could present further argument. The phone rang immediately after and she ignored it. She wasn't going to argue the point. The fresh air would help her feel better. Jogging was something she enjoyed and something that she hadn't done since the attack. Getting back into familiar routines was critical to recovery. The therapist had told her so and she agreed. Routine would remind her that, despite what had happened, she wasn't a victim and the incident shouldn't define her.

She jogged in place, then did some stretches. And as she did, a sense of déjà vu ran through her and she wondered if this might be a mistake. She shrugged off the feeling. The outdoors, fresh air and a bit of freedom were calling to her. After all, what could happen on a street she knew well where not a car had gone by in almost an hour. She couldn't be any safer. She pushed the doubts from her mind and went to get her sneakers.

Chapter Eleven

Travis's phone buzzed once.

"You've got trouble," Serene said without hesitation. "There's an intruder at your client's condo. I had a visual on the surveillance camera. Gangly, wearing a black hoodie. In the last few seconds they've slipped off the monitor. I didn't get much of a look. Couldn't determine sex, age, nothing."

"I saw the intruder earlier. I'm already on my way," Travis said. "Thanks for the details."

"It's worse. Just prior to that the client phoned me. She told me that she is going jogging."

"What? Tell me you stopped her. When did this happen?"

"I told her not to do it. But she disconnected before I could make a convincing argument. It was immediately after that that I got the visual on the intruder." Her voice was laced with frustration and concern. "Since then, I've called her numerous times. She's not answering."

"Where's Devon?" he growled out the question. While he hadn't given the order for twenty-four-hour surveillance yet, it was still expected that the marshals were twenty-four-seven in touch. Devon had been free to go for a break, thirty minutes or so at a time. What he hadn't been free to do was be out of contact.

As far as the twenty-four-hour surveillance, that was new and the onus was on him to let his men know. He'd been on his way to do that. In the meantime, Devon needed to be answering his phone. He'd been going back to Kiera's property anyway, he'd tell Devon then. A delay of minutes wasn't a concern, or so he'd thought at the time. It seemed only minutes ago when Kiera had contacted him to let him know everything was fine. She'd been reading a book, relaxed. Everything was okay.

"Have you contacted Devon?"

"I tried. No answer," Serene replied with frustration lacing her words. "I don't like this. One of them should be answering their phone. Something's wrong."

His heart thumped at the scene she was painting. He could only guess at why Kiera had contacted Serene instead of Devon or him. But why hadn't she contacted Devon or him instead? Why had she said she was reading a book one minute and then phoned Serene to say she was going jogging? Even as he asked the question, he knew the answer. The book was a smoke screen. He wouldn't have been as easy as Serene to skirt around. He would have demanded that she put the notion of jogging aside well before she'd had the opportunity to hang up. In fact, he would have anticipated that reaction, and he would have laid down the law before she'd ever stated her purpose. He would have used her own suspicions against her, and he knew that would have stopped her.

"Damn," Travis said. The curse was mild and didn't make him feel any better. He wanted to say so much worse and that wouldn't change anything either. He took a breath. They needed a physical presence, to stand between Kiera and danger.

"There's been nothing in the last thirty seconds or so," Serene said.

"I've got this." He disconnected and at the same time bore down on the accelerator. He was speeding in an area that was industrial, free of pedestrians, where he wouldn't endanger anyone. But, within minutes, he was back in a residential area and again had to watch his speed.

He gripped the wheel, his palms sweaty, his lips tight. Where was she? What was she doing? Was she safe or… He couldn't think of the latter, of the possibilities.

She was in danger with no one to defend her. Her bag had never been found. There'd been a death threat. Was it possible that someone knew where she lived? It was no question. Time was against him but despite that, he knew that he had to get there in time to intervene. He had the wheel in a death grip. That she'd gone against his advice was more than frustrating. At the same time, he realized why she'd done it. She was going stir crazy. He would feel the same in her situation. But he hoped all that didn't make her feel that it was worth the risk. Still, he could picture her checking the neighborhood, seeing no one and feeling safe. Odds were she was but he wasn't good with odds.

This was his fault. He should have realized that she needed to get out. That she needed to do something other than sit in her condo. He should have facilitated that, arranged safe outings in order to prevent this situation from happening.

He was as close to panic as he'd ever been. He called Kiera again. It was the third time. Like the other calls, it went straight to voice mail. He bit back his frustration. There was someone casing her condo and neither she nor Devon were answering their phones.

"Sweet hell," Travis muttered under his breath. He sped up when he could. And, within seconds, again found himself easing off the accelerator. He coasted through a red light on a street that was empty of other vehicles or pedestrians. He ordered Siri to dial Devon again. The phone rang and rang—no one answered.

Frustrated, he slammed the palm of his hand against the steering wheel. Two blocks and he turned the corner heading for a route where speed would not be an issue. Just as he thought that, a cargo truck pulled out in front of him.

He swore again as he swerved around the three-quarter-ton lumber truck. Minutes passed, and the distance closed. Five more blocks. Five blocks of not knowing if she was safe or what might be happening.

A murderer could very well be about to take another victim.

He couldn't think of any other reason why the trespasser was there. He didn't believe in coincidence. He didn't believe in a lot of things. But what he believed right now scared him like nothing ever had. Kiera's life was in danger. He knew that instinctively. That was one thing he never questioned, his instincts.

He took the corner at a speed that laid rubber on the pavement. Two blocks to go. A woman walking her dog stepped out and he swerved around them. He could see her in the rearview mirror. She was pumping her fist at him with the dog yanking on its lead and barking at him. He slowed down. He gripped the wheel, his lips compressed.

Two more blocks.

Would he be too late? The thought of that repeated like a metronome in his head, the beat dull and relentless, moving toward possible doom.

He couldn't be too late. He had to make it on time.

He couldn't believe that this was happening. He'd made his last drive by Kiera's place at eleven o'clock last night. At that time, he'd run into Devon and been given a bit of a hard time about getting too attached to a client, and about stepping in when he wasn't needed. He was right. He didn't need to be there. It was Devon's shift. As a result, he'd taken the ribbing as it was meant—joking laced with truth. He and Devon went a long way back. They'd gone to the university together and been friends ever since.

He dialed Devon's phone again. No answer.

If something happened to her…or Devon… It was a possibility he hadn't considered until now. But it was Kiera he worried about most. She was the target.

He had to remain focused. He took the last corner with a screech of tires.

KIERA HADN'T LIKED the FBI contact's reaction to her phone call. She didn't like being told what to do or not do. She hadn't called to get their permission. She'd called only as a courtesy. Despite the threatening phone calls, she felt safe in her own house and in her own neighborhood. She hadn't been out alone, or at all, since she'd welcomed Travis to the neighborhood. She smiled as she remembered that greeting. Her gun in his face wasn't exactly welcoming. Fortunately, Devon had had a more civilized introduction.

But all that was behind her. Now she was sick of her restrictions. Staying indoors had been fine those first days but now she'd begun to feel slightly claustrophobic. It was either get outside or go insane. She had a bad case of cabin fever.

The neighbor's dog was quiet. She'd used him as a barometer since she'd moved in. If there was a stranger in the area, he barked. She could usually hear him even if he was inside. The silence gave her comfort. Nothing was afoot, at least nothing that the dog had sensed. And, even if it was, she had her gun. It was in the gun belt that she'd purchased when she'd first inherited the weapon. The last time she'd worn it had been to the shooting range. It could be used two different ways, concealed and unconcealed. It could hide quite nicely under a T-shirt worn near the belt-line, so she wouldn't be frightening the neighbors with an in-your-face weapon. And she wouldn't be unarmed either.

She looked at her watch. Devon had told her that he'd be back in half an hour. That was forty-five minutes ago.

She bent down to make sure her shoelace was tied. It was time to reclaim her life, one little piece at a time.

Chapter Twelve

Travis felt as if time had run out. He couldn't stop the panicked feeling of doom. It was like nothing he'd felt before. And even though he was close to Kiera's condo, he wasn't close enough.

Every minute made the possibility that Kiera was injured or worse, all the more real. He needed to floor the accelerator and yet he couldn't. Running over a pedestrian or causing an accident wasn't the answer. Two tragedies would not fix anything.

Kiera.

Was she safe? What had happened since the last time he'd spoken to her? He tried to keep his mind off the possibilities. But his mind wouldn't stop reeling through the what-ifs and might-have-beens. He was afraid that he'd be too late. He couldn't take his mind off that possibility.

He parked at the end of the avenue that met with her street. He couldn't take the SUV any farther, not without making his presence known to whoever was lurking around her unit. From here he could see down her street. There was no activity, no cars, no people. Despite everything, despite a heartbeat that was revved for action, on the street everything appeared normal. He closed the driver's door with a controlled shut meant to be soundless. For he didn't know where the intruder might be or if they were gone. He went in on foot, across the lawn along the outside of the condos. Each building was three stories with two units on every floor. Her unit was on the main floor. As he moved along, he scoured the area for movement, for anything out of the ordinary.

Nothing.

Her building was in the middle of the block and the intruder could be anywhere, if he was here at all. Not even a dog's bark broke the silence. There was no one in sight as he came closer to her unit. There was nothing to indicate trouble.

Kiera might already be injured or worse. He needed her safe. He wouldn't have it any other way and yet his mind was already going to much more dire possibilities. The intruder had broken into her place. He should have called her, warned her. Kiera injured—dead, the unwanted possibility ran through his mind.

Not possible. Anger fueled his denial. He refocused his thoughts, focusing on the situation only, factoring emotion out of it. This was business first— emotion had no place, never had—and even now, he told himself futilely, it never would.

He had his gun in both hands. There were few people home now. He'd done the research days earlier. The block included not only the condos but single-family homes across the street. Most of the residents on the block were daytime workers of various kinds. The mix of people included six middle school children and two high schoolers. They were gone for the day. The others, four seniors, one unemployed and one night worker, were in the minority and what they might think should they look out a shuttered window was not a consideration. As long as they stayed indoors, there was no problem. He cleared his mind as he moved across front lawns, keeping under cover as much as possible until he was at her condo. There was nothing out of the ordinary. The blinds were down as he'd told Kiera to keep them. The condos on either side were silent; the driveways were empty. But none of that was unusual, it was a working-class neighborhood and it was the middle of the day. Outside, there was no sign of Kiera. Was she out jogging as she'd said she would be?

He moved along the perimeter. He needed to make sure the area was safe, the threat gone before he checked on her. There was a bank of shrubs on the west side of the building. It was an end unit, so whoever had been casing her place could well have moved around or even be inside. His grip tightened on the gun handle and anger was white-hot in his gut at the thought that someone might be threatening her. But there was no sign of forced entry from the front. That left the back. He turned to go in that direction and that's when he sensed something was off. That's when the small hairs rose on the back of his neck and he felt that he wasn't alone.

SOMETHING WASN'T RIGHT.

The feeling had been strong enough for Kiera to give up the idea of jogging more than five minutes ago. She'd done one circuit of the block and stopped midway through a second. A feeling of déjà vu and a chill swept through her at the same time. Everything felt still, too still, and a knot had formed in her gut as she felt as if she'd been transported to a place she'd been before—a dark, frightening place. The quiet, the feeling of being alone and the only person outside had overwhelmed her and she'd ended her jog. There was something not right and her instincts screamed for her to return home. If there was one thing she'd learned after the nightmare she'd survived was to follow her instinct. So instead of continuing her jog, she'd gone inside where she'd double-checked the door locks, front and back. Then, she put her sneakers away. In her socked feet, she went to the bedroom, opened the nightstand and took her aunt's gun from under her t-shirt. She hesitated before putting it away. The weapon felt foreign and cold in her hand; even the memories it invoked of her aunt were gone. A chill ran through her, for nothing seemed as it should be. Something was shifting, something dark and gray and… Something was very wrong. Her intuition was in overdrive. She opened the drawer and took the gun back out.

With her other hand, she reached for her phone. The prepaid Travis had gotten for her was so small in comparison to her smartphone that she'd forgotten twice where she'd put it. Now it was gone, again.

She frowned. She traced her steps back. Her mind had been on Devon's phone and how he'd forgotten it. She hadn't been thinking about where she'd placed her phone and now she couldn't remember where she'd set it. With her mind on the missing phone, she placed the gun on the end table.

"Irresponsible," she muttered.

She glanced around and got down on her hands and knees. Finally, she found it under the couch cushions where, if anyone had called, she'd never have heard it. She guessed that it had slipped out of her pocket after she'd called and alerted the woman in charge of her surveillance of her intent to go jogging. She'd been sitting on the couch when she'd made the call and she'd thought that she'd slipped the phone into her pocket. Obviously, it had slipped out.

She looked out the window. Nothing had changed and yet her gut was tight and strumming like a wrong note playing again and again. She looked at her watch. Devon had left to grab lunch and assured her he'd be back in thirty minutes or less. If there was trouble, as she sensed now, she'd phone Travis. He was her go-to man anyway, the one she depended on. The truth was there'd been something building between them from the very beginning.

"What the hell are you thinking, girl?" she chastised herself. She was acting like a woman in love, or more aptly in lust, rather than a woman in crisis.

The street was silent. The last vehicle she had seen seemed like forever ago. It had belonged to a neighbor at the end of the block. She turned and put the gun on the end table. There was no threat. It had been her imagination. She was overreacting again. But she couldn't help it. She'd been through things that most people never face in a lifetime. She needed time. She knew that. She went to the kitchen to grab a cup of coffee. She added a dash of sugar to the dark brew and carried the drink back to the living area. Seconds ticked slowly by and felt like minutes. She set the coffee down by the gun.

She picked up a book. Despite the fact that it was the latest cozy mystery by her favorite author, it held no interest. Somehow reading about crime of any sort wasn't comforting. But she needed something to do. She'd cleaned the house thoroughly two days ago and there wasn't a dust ball anywhere. She thought of Prairie Seniors' Care Home and realized how much she missed the work and the people.

She was itching to go back, to be useful again. She smiled as Lucy wove herself between her legs with a deep, satisfied purr. Then the cat leaped up beside her and curled up for a nap. She thought of the cat's easy nature and how she'd settled quickly into her new home. Now, six months later, they were a team—both considered each other family, or so Kiera would like to think.

She looked at her watch. Two minutes had gone by and it had seemed like forever. She was feeling particularly anxious and she wasn't sure why. She'd opened the blinds at an angle that she could see out, but no one could see in. It was against Travis's warning. But she needed to see what was going on—so far nothing.

Something moved at the edge of her condo. She didn't have a full view from her window and her heart raced before relief rushed through her.

Travis.

She'd recognize him anywhere.

He was near the cotoneaster shrub a few feet from her main entrance.

She frowned.

His back was to her and she sensed that something was wrong. Just the way he held himself, the way he hadn't come to her door as soon as he'd arrived. That wasn't normal. Usually he came immediately to check on her. Something was up.

She thought of stepping out, asking him what was going on, why he was here. But then something else caught her attention. There was a movement in the opposite direction. She caught it from the corner of her eye. She crouched down so the window ledge was now at eye level and she was at the corner of the window frame—out of sight. She watched but the movement didn't repeat and there was nothing and no one in sight.

Her heart seemed to knock in her rib cage and her hands shook as something intuitive told her that Travis wasn't the only one on her front lawn. Someone else who he hadn't seen was there, hidden by shrubbery. Maybe it was the neighbor's cat, but instinct told her it wasn't. Her heart thumped at the thought that Travis might be in danger.

Something shifted and nothing was the same. Now she could see who was at the other end of her unit. She could see the top of a faded black hoodie. Whoever they were, they were almost the length of her unit from Travis and they were definitely shadowing him and moving closer. It was also clear the way they kept furtively to the bushes, that they didn't want to be seen. Obviously, they were up to no good. They were hunched over. And she couldn't see their face.

The faded black garment was too big and sagged over their frame. Male or female, it was impossible to tell. She backed up from the corner of the window where she'd been peeking out. She bit back the tremor that ran through her. She had to warn Travis and yet she knew that as soon as she opened that front door she'd make his stalker aware of her presence. That might put Travis in as much danger as he was now, maybe more. As she contemplated her choices, the stalker disappeared from sight. Her heart was locked in her throat.

She had to do something. Knocking on the window would alert them both. With Travis at a disadvantage, unaware of whoever was stalking him, that wasn't the answer. It was up to her to protect him. She didn't think for a minute of the irony of that thought. Instead, she raced to the table and grabbed the gun. She fumbled with the safety as she hurried to the door. She'd never felt so nervous. Life and death weighed on her shoulders. She could almost hear the pounding of her heart. Her fingers wouldn't cooperate as they slipped on the lock, finally unlocking it with one hand while holding the gun with the other.

She opened the door and it was then that she saw that she was already too late. Travis's stalker was to his left, screened by shrubbery. The person had a metal bar raised high over their head and was standing directly behind him but out of his line of vision. Only a few feet separated them.

Everything was happening so fast, too fast. None of it was real and it was occurring in blips of time that were less than seconds and felt so much longer. The metal bar was coming down about to hit Travis's head. The stalker turned, looking at her as Kiera froze. She knew she didn't have a clear shot, not one that didn't run the risk of shooting Travis. In the strange tableau that seemed to be moving slowly through a fog, the hoodie slipped and partially revealed braided gray-streaked black hair and the face of a middle-aged woman.

No! Her scream was silent. Her throat seemed closed, her broken voice frozen in fear. There was only one option. She had to take the woman out. But she had no time to line up the shot. She had to make do with a quick shot, a warning shot and hope it was enough. She held the gun with shaking hands and fired. At the same time, metal flashed; a crowbar or something like it was swinging at Travis's head.

Travis crumpled to the ground. She fired again but the woman bolted across the lawn and disappeared from sight. It had all happened in seconds and yet it had seemed like forever.

Kiera's heart was in her throat and tears were in her eyes as she rushed to Travis's side.

She was too late.

"Travis, no!"

Her cry did nothing. He was dead and her heart broke.

Chapter Thirteen

Kiera dropped to her knees beside Travis.

She was terrified. She feared he was dead. And even if he wasn't, the danger wasn't over. She clutched the gun in one shaking hand like it was a lifeline. But, as her aunt had promised so long ago, the gun had been a game changer. She'd scared off his attacker with it, even stopped the attack. Except it hadn't been enough.

She took a breath, stilling the first rush of fear. Her professional instincts were kicking in. This was a medical emergency and she'd dealt with these before. She couldn't think the worst. She could only deal with the present. He had to be alive.

She was frozen in place at the thought, the very idea that he might not survive. She needed to check his pulse. She had to take charge of this situation. She took a deep breath as if needing courage before reaching for his wrist. But she'd barely touched it, felt the heat of his skin against hers and she dropped it.

This wasn't like her. She didn't hesitate. She'd handled many medical crises in her short career. But this was different. This was Travis. She was scared for the worst and because of that she didn't want to know the truth. She didn't want to know that there was no hope. None of that was an excuse. She pushed back into a squat that put inches of space between them.

Your auntie raised no coward.

It was a mantra she'd lived by in the years since her aunt's funeral. That mantra had seen her through the last few teenage years alone. Without the guidance of her aunt, she'd made the journey to get a profession, become an adult and stand on her own two feet, alone. Now this was on her, on no one else. Whether he was alive or dead, she needed to take care of this. She reached for his wrist and felt for a pulse. The strong beat almost took her breath away.

He was alive.

She was overwhelmed with relief and memories. Only yesterday when she'd teased him. Only a few mornings ago, he'd been with her as they listened to the phone call that had terrified her and threatened her life. She thought of how he'd held her after the first phone call and just before the life-threatening phone call.

He'd been there for her in more ways than he needed to be.

Now he needed help. But he needed more than a nurse-practitioner who had no medical equipment on hand had to offer. As she thought that, a familiar vehicle took the corner onto the driveway too fast and skidded to a stop. Relief flooded through her as Devon leaped out, slammed the car door and bolted up the driveway. His revolver was in both hands, and there was a look of intense determination on his face as the gun moved left and right as if trolling for danger.

"He was attacked," she said. "By someone with a metal bar."

Devon had both hands on his gun, ready for anything.

"Where are they?"

"Disappeared around the house."

Devon holstered the gun and was down on his knees beside her.

"Is he…?"

"He's alive and his pulse is strong," she broke in before he could ask the question that had only so recently terrified her. "He was hit on the back of the head."

"How the hell did this happen?" Devon asked. "The area was clear before I left."

She shook her head and stood up. She had no answers. She hardly knew herself what had happened. She only knew what she'd seen.

"Where did they come from?"

"From that direction," she pointed in the opposite direction. "I caught a glimpse from the window." Her voice choked but she pushed on. "There was no chance to warn him." There was more. There was one detail that could change everything. She held back, not sure how Devon or even Travis would react.

"I was too late," she said instead with honest and sincere regret.

She shivered. The air was cool and hinted at the possibility of rain.

Devon reached down and took Travis's phone from his back pocket.

Kiera's legs felt suddenly weak. She dropped to her knees beside Travis.

"Thanks, Serene, I'll keep you posted." Devon finished his conversation and squatted down beside Kiera. "I'm going to make sure the area is clear. Serene has an ambulance on the way. You're alright here?"

She nodded and barely glanced up as Devon left them.

"Travis," she whispered in his ear as she bent close to him. She barely knew him and yet she knew that it would tear out her heart to lose him.

She felt along his skull, feeling for injury and also noticing the soft texture of his hair. It was short, cropped off not in a stylish way, but one that was practical, one that fit his profession. Her hand went as far to the back as it could, her fingers gently probing. She felt what she presumed was blood. She pulled her hand free. Head wounds tended to bleed profusely. Her hand was bloody. But that told her only what she already knew, that he'd been hit on the back of the head. He could have a concussion. The seriousness of that could only be determined by medical tests like an X-ray.

She stood up, swinging around at the sound of footsteps behind her.

"I'm sorry—I didn't mean to frighten you," Devon

said. He looked down at Travis. "I don't understand what happened. Did he scare off the intruder before?"

"No," Kiera interrupted him. "He never saw his attacker."

"Never saw— Then how?"

"There was an intruder, armed with a steel bar," Kiera said breathlessly, barely looking at him before turning back to Travis.

"How long ago?"

"A minute, maybe two," she replied. "Whoever it was disappeared. I think they went around the corner of the condo. I'm not sure. I…" Her voice broke.

"I fired a couple of shots but I was too late. The stalker snuck up on him." She looked at the gun with regret. "I never got a clear shot. My shots may have scared them off. I don't know."

"Good work."

Relief flooded through Kiera at the sound of Travis's voice. It was husky and quieter than she knew it to be. It didn't matter. He was not only alive but conscious.

"Ouch," he said as he sat up. His hand went to the back of his head and came back, as hers had, smeared with blood.

"Crap, you're bleeding, man," Devon said.

"What the hell happened?" Travis asked.

"You were hit on the back of the head," Kiera said. "They snuck up behind you."

"That explains it," he said in a dry tone that in another situation might be an attempt at humor. "My head hurts like it's about to explode."

"We'll get you to the hospital," Kiera said. She took his arm as if she might help him up.

"No!" He pulled away. "No," he repeated less forcefully.

"There's an ambulance en route," Kiera said.

"I'll be fine."

"Once you're looked at, maybe," she replied.

"Unbelievable, this shouldn't have happened," Devon said. "I should have been here."

"You couldn't have known," she said. "No one did."

"Someone could have," Travis snarled as he struggled to his feet. "Where were you?" he asked glaring at Devon.

"The area was secure. At least I thought so," Devon said. "I screwed up."

"You're not kidding," Travis took a step forward, the look on his face like he was going to punch the other man.

Kiera grabbed Travis's arm. "We misjudged. I told him to go, to take a break. He's allowed breaks. I remember you saying so."

"No, Kiera. This is on me," Devon said.

"No," Kiera said. "It isn't. It was my choice, my insistence. I felt comfortable and I'm not about to run and you knew it. That was the only reason you were here, to make sure I didn't run. At least that's what I thought until now."

"Where were you?" Travis asked Devon. "A break is one thing man, but you were gone a lot longer. You were out of contact. You…"

"Completely and totally screwed up. I dropped my phone and didn't know it was missing. And by the time I realized it I'd already ordered my lunch. The food was delayed…"

"Let me get this straight," he interrupted. "You waited for your food rather than get your ass back here for your phone."

"Travis, please. It's alright. I'm not going anywhere. You know that. It's not his fault," Kiera pleaded. "No one could have predicted an intruder…"

The scowl on Devon's face said otherwise. She wished that she could ease the guilt that she knew he was feeling. While he hadn't spent the time with her that Travis had, she liked him.

"Damn it, I hold you responsible, but I blame myself as well," Travis said. "It was my call. I told you to take breaks."

"I took a break as you'd agreed and I was gone longer than I'd said," Devon replied. "A lot longer. And dropping the phone…"

"Was a major screwup," Travis replied.

"I found it after you left," Kiera added.

"There's nothing I can say except it won't happen again," Devon said.

"It better not," Travis replied. "You reported it?"

"I did. The least I could do considering…" Devon said. "You'd be right to have me removed from the case."

"Don't tempt me," Travis said. "You called it in? I thought your phone was missing."

"I borrowed yours and notified Serene of the incident. Catch," Devon said as he tossed the phone.

Travis caught it easily in one hand.

Devon glanced at Kiera with a crooked grin. "I think our boy might be right. He'll be fine."

"I hope so," Kiera said. She agreed that his eye-hand coordination seemed unaffected.

"Is the area clear?" Travis asked.

"Yeah," Devon replied. "I checked inside and nothing around her unit, front or back. I just did a cursory of the outside, but I'm going to take another look at the perimeter," Devon said to Travis. He headed across the lawn, widening the scope of his first search.

Kiera struggled to hold back tears. He could have died. She could have died. Death had again stared her in the face. Worse, it had almost taken him from her. She didn't know if she could have survived that.

"Kiera?" His voice was softer, deeper than normal. It was as if speaking was an effort. And she imagined, considering what had happened, that it was. And yet he was still in the game, only minutes after taking a blow to the head.

She pushed a stray hair off her face as if that would focus her mind where it needed to be. And yet she didn't want to go there. She didn't know if she had the courage to go there. It was terrifying. For that place brought forth other possibilities. Like who and what his attacker might have been and why they were here at her condo. Had Travis just been in the way? Had they been trying to get to her? Was she a danger to everyone she knew and everyone she cared about?

Travis sat down. Sweat gleamed on his forehead.

"You need to stay seated and let your head clear," she said and couldn't help the chastising tone of her voice. She was relieved to put her attention, at least temporarily, to medical matters.

He grabbed her hand and pulled her down toward him. "I'll be fine," he said with steel in his voice. He pulled her closer. His hand was hot against her wrist. There was a hint of the shaving cream he'd used that morning that seemed to curl around her. The scent of him reminded her of early morning and lemons.

The grounds were quiet. Devon was coming around the corner. He was on the opposite side of her unit. And from the look on his face, he hadn't found any more information than they already had.

Travis ran the back of his palm across his forehead. "Did you see anything else? Anything?"

The questions were a relief to Kiera. For despite the fact that he was conscious and speaking, she didn't know how badly he was injured. A head injury was always frightening. His questions showed that he was not only aware of what happened, but that the hit on the head hadn't scrambled his brains.

"It all happened so quickly. You could have died. I should have…"

"You should have done nothing more than you already did. Without you I'd be dead."

She shook her head. "I should have shot sooner. I should have…"

"You probably didn't have a clear shot and you're not a marksman, so you waited," Travis said. "Understandable. But despite all that, you saved my life. If you hadn't been there, I would have been dead. There's no question of that. Don't doubt yourself. I can only say thank you."

"Don't thank me…"

"There's no one else to thank. I'm not sure how or what happened, how I missed it. But I'm alive because of you."

"If I'd…"

"Stop." He held up a hand. "Tell me what you saw but no more about it being your fault. It's not." He paused as if for emphasis. "You did everything you could."

Kiera took a deep breath. "She hit you in the back of the head. It looked like she used a crowbar. That's my best guess. The sun was glinting and making it hard to see."

"She?" Devon said. He'd just returned from his search of the area. "Are you suggesting that his attacker was female?"

She swallowed back all the resistance and pushback that she knew was to come. It was time to stand her ground, speak of what she knew. "Yes. A woman, middle-aged. I caught a glimpse of her face."

"Where are you going with this?" Travis asked.

"Don't you see? There's a connection between my kidnapping, the phone calls and this." Kiera said with determination and frustration lacing her voice. "There were two killers, exactly as I told you. And one of them is back to get me."

Chapter Fourteen

"Are you alright?" Travis asked a few minutes later when they were inside her condo.

"I'm fine," Kiera assured him. "It's you we're worried about." She'd waited outside on her stoop as he'd spoken privately to Devon and then put in a phone call to the local police. Since then the ambulance had arrived. They'd pulled into the driveway with lights and sirens off as requested. The paramedics had checked the head wound, cleaned it up and agreed with her assessment. Although all parties agreed they'd prefer if he followed up. And again, Travis refused. But at least there was a consensus that odds were he had no concussion and he'd had on the spot treatment from professionals with equipment she didn't have access to.

He glanced at Devon and she didn't miss the subtle nod they exchanged.

"I'll check the neighborhood," Devon said.

Silence filled the room for a few seconds after Devon left.

"How's your head?"

"Fine," Travis said.

"I'll get you some water," she said, for his voice sounded choked, hoarse even.

"Did you get a good look at who did it?" he asked after she'd returned a minute later and seconds after he'd taken a swallow of the water she'd brought him.

She shook her head. "Kind of yes and kind of no. It was a quick look and I saw only part of her face."

"Tell me again what you saw?" he said. "The details."

She sat down beside him and he took her hands in his.

She held on to his hands tight as the image of that face flooded her memory. "Long black hair, streaked with gray, and braided. I think she was middle aged, her face was tanned and lined. At least the part of her face that I saw. I never made eye contact. She turned away in just a split second."

"I know you only remember seeing one of your kidnappers. But was there anything familiar about her? Anything that triggered a memory?"

And they both knew what he was asking. Was she the elusive second kidnapper?

She shivered. "I only heard him. At least, I thought it was a man, but the voice—" she frowned "—could have been either male or female. That's all I have and your attacker didn't speak, and I didn't completely see her face."

His hand turned hers over and his thumb stroked her palm. The action was both surprising and comforting, and completely not the Travis she knew. He tried his best to keep their relationship professional.

As if reading her thoughts, he squeezed her hand and let go. "We'll talk about this later. In the meantime, I need to report what happened today."

He stood up, pulling her to her feet. "You'll be okay for an hour or so? Devon will be here. This time he won't be leaving. And there'll be a police cruiser in the area. I won't be long, but I need to file the report on this. I'll send a sketch artist here and let Devon know to expect them."

"No worries," she said. "The question is, are you okay?"

"I'm fine," he said as she walked with him to the door. He opened it and stood in the doorway, looking at her as if contemplating something about her, or the situation or both. She wasn't sure what was going through his mind.

"Kiera..." His voice dropped off as if he were considering what he wanted to say or even how he was going to say it.

"What?" she asked.

"I just want you to know, that I'm completely behind you. We have one killer behind bars but I know that there's someone else out there. Whether this was her or not, we'll get them sooner or later, Kiera. One killer at a time."

She shivered. "She found me." It was as much a question as it was at statement.

"Maybe, but she's at a disadvantage. You've seen her and you'll never be alone."

"I have my gun. I'll keep the doors locked and..."

She looked at him, remembered that he'd been wounded protecting her. "You be careful too!"

He touched her cheek. "Call me if you need me, if you're scared at all—anything. We'll make sure you're safe. Promise."

"What about you?" she asked.

"I'll be alright," he said and the look in his eyes said he appreciated her concern. "You worry too much," he said as he pushed a strand of hair that had escaped her ponytail back from her cheek. He took her by the waist, pulling her closer to him. "I like that."

"Do you?" she said in a voice that was soft, almost provocative.

For heaven's sake, she thought, *you're flirting with the man who almost died protecting you*. It was an outrageous thought. Yet, she wanted nothing but to run her hands along the firm lines of his body.

She didn't have any warning when he kissed her. It was hot and hard and wet all at the same time. It was passion and the promise of more. It was the perfect kiss as she melted into him, kissing him back, mating her tongue with his. She fit against him like they were meant to be. She ached for this kiss to never end, for it to become more.

But with it came the knowledge that in the aftermath of what had happened, nothing could come of this. She pulled away. She needed to keep her head straight, her wits about her, and so did he.

"Go. You've got work to do," she said in a voice

that didn't sound like hers at all. It felt strange and distant, and far from sincere. "Go," she encouraged.

He looked at her strangely as if he didn't believe what she was saying. And then a curtain seemed to come down and there was a distance between them again. It was like a professional space that breached the growing personal connection. She breathed a sigh of relief. That was the truth of their relationship. She was a client or a case, whatever it was that marshals called their assignments—nothing more.

Travis looked at his smartwatch. "Give me an hour, no more, and I'll be back. You'll be okay?" he repeated as if repetition would assure that she would be.

"I'll be fine," she said. She pointed to the end table where her gun lay. "I have the old standby, Devon and apparently part of the police department." It was a relief to know that he trusted her and knew she wasn't going to take off. This was the safest place she could be.

"You do."

"I'm not worried," she said. "Do what you need to."

"I DON'T LIKE THIS," James said twenty minutes later. "Especially the fact that you were attacked. Damn it, you could have been killed."

"I'm fine," Travis assured him once again.

James shoved back in his chair and stood up. "That's the one good thing to come out of this conversation. The rest…" He shook his head. "The two-kidnapper theory, the fact that no evidence of their existence was ever found over an almost fourteen-month investigation, seems implausible. Except, and here's where I contradict myself, there's been too much happening for it not to all be related. I just can't get over the fact that one killer may have flown so far under the radar."

"Except now they're out and not so quiet," Travis said. "The phone calls, the attack on me—casing Kiera's place. All of it. What if Kiera's right? What if the one that got away is now after her?"

It was a question for which they didn't have the answer. But he needed to talk this out. The theory of two killers, the attack—all of it added up to a threat to their witness, a threat to Kiera.

"We can't dismiss the idea that we don't have this case locked up," Travis said.

James frowned. "I don't like anything that came down this afternoon. Especially that I can't marry any of these incidents up to solid facts. I don't want any of this affecting her testimony."

"It won't. With any luck we'll have the pair of them locked up well before then."

"Sounds like best case scenario. If there are two killers. Otherwise, if they're all separate events then we have a variety of crimes happening and only one commonality—Kiera. All the crime happens around her. All the crime happens after she escapes the serial killer," James said slowly, contemplating the suggestion as if it had become fact. "Interesting, if we factor in the possibility that someone acquired leaked information."

"Not likely," Travis said.

"Agreed," James replied. "But a remote possibility."

"Never mind that—just look at the evidence. The phone calls, the stalker. You start piling the evidence together and it's adding up to a big something."

"Like I said, I can't disagree," James said slowly. "What I can say is that this is completely out of the ordinary. It's not the pattern that the average serial killer follows. Of course, there're exceptions, there always are. Even so, the specific cases of couples working together are rare. The Wests in England for one. But, in that case, she wasn't the dominant player, he was."

The more Travis thought about the recent events, the more convinced he became. But the more evidence they could gather, the better. He intended to sit down and talk to Kiera. The memories were still coming back, so the possibility of her remembering something new, something more tangible, in the next few days was a possibility. He knew the FBI would speak to her in the days leading up to the trial but somehow, he believed that he might have more success. She trusted him. In a way, the desire she ignited in him aside, they were friends.

"In the meantime, we know there's a threat—that fact no one disputes. So we need to move our witness to a safe house."

"I agree," Travis said with a feeling of relief. That was one item off the table. There was no discussion, done deal. He knew James would get that in the works and it was only a matter of alerting Kiera. He pushed that from his mind, knowing that convincing her might not be so easy. Despite her claims that another killer was still at large, she was anxious to go back to work and return to the life she'd put on pause since the incident. He'd convince her one way or another. He had no choice. What he had now was another issue—one almost as big as the one they'd just put to bed.

James leaned forward, his elbows on his desk. "I'm sensing another request in the works." He looked Travis in the eye as if forcing the point.

"I'd like to interview Eric Solomon," he said as he moved to the next item on his agenda.

"You'd like to what?" James said in a voice that was strained. It was a voice that barely held back his outrage at Travis's request. "What do you expect that will accomplish? He's already been interviewed and said next to nothing."

"I'm not sure," Travis said, unsurprised at the reaction. "Considering everything that's happened, the playing field has shifted."

"In your opinion."

Travis shrugged off the interruption. "Different questions, different interviewer, might get a different response. Maybe a different insight."

"You think he'll let something slip?"

"Maybe he can help us connect the dots."

"The odds are that he may say nothing at all," James said.

"True. But we also might gain some insight. Plus, he's had time to think. Maybe he'll reveal something that will give us that connection."

"Doubtful. While he hasn't lawyered up yet—that

doesn't mean he won't request one. And that will change everything. Right now, he's just refused."

Travis was silent for a second digesting that interesting piece of information. "That aside, it would be negligent not to let me interview."

"How so?"

"It's a shot. Something might have changed. I know it's changed for us. This assignment isn't what I expected and maybe Eric is willing to shed some light on it."

James was shaking his head.

"We have the chance of changing the odds," Travis finished as he saw the stormy look on James's face. "Especially sending someone like me in." He held up his hand, staving off James's interruption. "Why? Because, I wasn't part of the original arrest so I'm unknown to the perp. The bonus? I'm actively involved in the case. But he doesn't know that. I have an inside scoop on the possibility of a twist…"

"There is no twist," James said with gritted teeth. "At least none that has any backing."

"So, let me do it."

"I don't know, Travis."

"What will it hurt?"

James shrugged. "Fair enough. I don't think you can do any harm. Maybe this idea of there being a partner in these crimes is a theory that dies as a result of this interview. I can only hope, because that surely complicates things. In the meantime, maybe you're right, it definitely has the potential to change things—or not." He shrugged.

"Agreed. Fifteen minutes, that's all I ask."

In the hall a door slammed shut. Someone laughed. Silence settled thick and uneasy between them as they sat on either side of the old oak desk.

"Alright, fifteen minutes and not a minute more. I'll arrange it ASAP. Let's say tomorrow at ten o'clock."

Travis stood up. "Thanks," he said to his friend and, for the duration of this case, superior. It was an awkward situation but one that they so far were handling without injury to their friendship.

"Don't thank me yet. You could walk out of there looking like an idiot."

"I'll buy the round," Travis said. "But if I'm right…"

"No chance of that."

"If I'm right that changes everything."

"Agreed," James said with a frown. "We can both hope that the theory is as whacked as it sounds. Neither one of us needs this complication."

Travis didn't disagree. He hoped that James was right. And he prayed that Kiera was wrong, but he feared she was very right. If that was the case, there was another killer on the loose, exactly as she'd said. And this time, they might very well have Kiera in their sights.

Chapter Fifteen

Travis had already had two cups of coffee when he arrived the next morning in Rawlings, Wyoming. It was a little after nine thirty in the morning. The Rawlings State Penitentiary was where the notorious serial killer, Eric Solomon, was being held as he awaited trial.

It was Thursday, exactly fifteen minutes before ten, when Travis entered the facility. He immediately felt trapped, confined, as he always did within the walls of a prison. He hated this aspect of his job, for prisons always made him feel claustrophobic. There was no reason for the feeling, no past trauma or phobia that he could put his finger on. Maybe it was just a subconscious aversion at the thought of being confined.

He pushed the thoughts from his mind and went through clearance. He was then ushered to the interrogation room. He was fifteen minutes early. He'd planned that, for he'd known that by the time he cleared security and made the necessary pleasantries with the officials, he'd be right on time.

As he entered the room and the door clanged behind him, the noises of the prison fell away and he pulled out a chair and sat down. It was the position in which he began any interview with someone who was incarcerated. It was less threatening than standing. He glanced at his smartwatch to make sure he was still ahead of schedule and to mark his time. He was now five minutes early. From everything he knew from the file and what James had told him, the murderer had said little. As a result, the odds that he'd open up to Travis were slim, but he still had hope. That the possibility was there meant that he had to take it. He knew that was the reason James had agreed—the faint hope of information.

Five minutes later the metal door opened. A medium-sized man, with blond hair that curled over his ears and average looks, leaned nonchalantly against the doorframe. His face was boyish and younger looking than Travis had expected. Eric Solomon was only two months younger than he was and yet he looked a decade younger. His youthful face helped make him look trustworthy. It was what had lured too many women to their deaths.

Travis tried to maintain a friendly look while feeling nothing but loathing for this man who had brutally killed so many women. He had to clench his hands at his sides and struggle to keep a pleasant expression. This piece of crap had threatened Kiera, had touched her, torn her clothes and meant to violate and then kill her. He couldn't think of that, for the rage it built in him would become uncontrollable in seconds. He'd stand up and take this piece of trash's throat in his hands and…

Damn it, Johnson. Cool it.

He couldn't. He'd kill him for what he'd thought that he could do to the woman he cared about.

He took a mental step back. What the hell was he thinking? He didn't care about Kierra not in that way, not in a romantic way. He hated this piece of trash. That was it.

There was no getting around it. It was too soon. He didn't know her. It didn't matter. He was falling for her.

Focus, damn it.

The guard gave the man a push. Eric took another step inside. The step was reluctant, forced on him from behind. He gave Travis a bland look that showed little emotion as he was forced to take another step into the room by a second shove from the guard.

"Behave yourself," the guard ordered. "Fifteen minutes," he said as he looked at Travis.

Travis gave him a nod and the guard walked out closing the door behind him with a distinctive click.

Travis made a snap decision. He guessed that sitting for this interview wasn't going to work, or at least sitting and waiting for him to sit wasn't working. He needed to meet him halfway. Pride was standing between them and, to eliminate that problem, they needed to be on equal footing. He stood up and held out his hand.

"Eric?"

"Marshal Johnson," Eric said with a sarcastic look.

"Travis."

Just like that, Eric smiled at him, the previous antagonism gone.

Travis guessed it was an act not unlike his own.

"Have a seat," Travis said as he reached for his own chair.

Travis pulled out the chair, and he sat down.

So did Eric.

They did it almost in sync.

Travis watched the murderer with casual nonchalance. He didn't slouch in his chair. But he didn't sit up straight either. He did everything not to appear threatening. Now, facing the man who was accused of such horrendous things, he wondered what could have brought him to that while tamping down the feeling of outrage that Kiera had been so close to dying at this man's hand.

He took a breath and focused on objectivity. This was his one chance. He'd read the file. Eric Solomon had had every dysfunctional trigger necessary through his childhood to raise him into the killer he'd become. He was a classic case. He'd come from a fragmented and dysfunctional family. He had a father who had disappeared before he was six, a stepfather who had been abusive and a mother who'd been mostly absent.

Travis knew that children could overcome those odds; many did. Not Eric. He'd run away from home at thirteen and disappeared off the authorities' radar. Following that, there'd been a long period of silence, until now.

Although he'd seen the file picture, it didn't reflect what Travis saw now—an open, friendly face. It was an illusion, he knew that. The initial assessment had indicated that the suspect was a sociopath. It was clear that Eric was giving him what he thought he wanted.

Eric silently watched with obvious reluctance and then slouched as he faced Travis with his arms folded. His face was tense, resistant. He barely looked at Travis. In fact, he didn't look at anything at all except the top of the desk that separated them.

His well-toned frame made it clear that he spent a good deal of time working out. Travis wondered if he spent any time contemplating the lives he had taken. He guessed the opposite might be true, that he might think about taking more. Fortunately, he could no longer do that. The question remained, was there someone out there who could. Someone who would carry on where he'd left off? Was Kiera's theory valid at all? Was what he and James speculated a reality?

"You killed a lot of people, Eric," he said without inflection. He slouched back in his chair. He didn't make eye contact but rather looked over the man's shoulder. His words were designed to be exactly as they sounded, unimpressed.

"You been living under a rock?" Eric snarled. "That's old news."

"You're right, it is," Travis replied, deciding to go straight for the heart. "Bet you wish that traitor who rode along with you got some justice too."

Silence met that comment.

Eric's lips tightened. His eyes flicked right and

then left and didn't quite meet his. Travis pulled back in his chair as if putting as much distance as possible between them.

Seconds ticked by and Eric slouched further down in his seat as if by that he were proving his disinterest.

"You've been wronged. I can see that," Travis said knowing that the sudden changes in mood were on the accused murderer's file. He was extremely unpredictable.

Silence filled the room and seconds ticked by.

Eric shifted on the rock-hard metal chair. He glanced at the clock on the wall. Then he leaned forward, an ugly look on his face as if he were about to physically attack.

"Where is she? Where is the bitch that put me here?"

Travis didn't say anything immediately. He didn't want to give Eric Kiera's name.

"If she's not dead yet, she will be soon." He shook his head and his next words put all doubts to rest. "I should have raped her when I had the chance."

At that, it took everything Travis had not to lunge across the table and choke the life from this piece of crap. He'd dealt with a lot of slime in his time but never had it been so personal.

"Got under your skin, didn't I? Tell me where she is and maybe I'll tell you a bit more of what you want?"

He wouldn't let Eric see how much the turn in conversation had gotten to him. Instead he flipped the interrogation back to where it belonged—on the killer.

"Would you have started killing without him, Eric?" He asked, taking charge of the interview. He didn't wait for an answer. He held the killer's eyes as if the truth might be hidden there. "You weren't alone, were you?"

Eric cursed.

"Your partner was the reason that you got into this mess wasn't he, Eric?"

He'd been winging it for the last few minutes, relying on the fact that there might be some hate on Eric's part over what had happened to him. That was, if any of this had any validity, if the relationship existed at all, if there was another killer.

He met the accused serial killer's insolent gaze with a "couldn't care less" look of his own. Eyes told a lot about someone. In this case, the accused's eyes were a dusty blue, innocent as a baby's except there didn't seem to be any depth to them. They reflected the overhead fluorescent light: flat, barren—emotionless. Travis sat back, stretching his legs out, keeping his arms free, his hands on the desk.

"So, now they're free and you're here. This isn't what you deserve."

"I don't know what you're talking about."

Travis ignored that. "What do you think? I think he has himself a new partner, someone else to enjoy his pursuits with."

Silence was thick in the room. The dull clang of metal echoed down the hall. Eric's mouth tightened. His arms folded across his chest as he leaned back.

Whether on purpose or by accident, he was copying Travis's pose.

Precious seconds ticked by; a minute passed. And then, just as he prepared to launch his attack from another angle, Eric sat up and leaned forward. His expressionless eyes, eyes that made Travis want to take a step back, met his.

"She deserves to die alongside me," Eric muttered.

She.

That one word seemed to vibrate between them. He couldn't believe what he'd just heard. It was amazing that he'd revealed anything at all, Travis thought. He pushed that reaction back, concentrating on keeping his face emotionless.

"I can understand that feeling," Travis said.

Eric said nothing.

"We're close to making that happen, but we need your help to do it," Travis said ignoring the animosity that felt alive between them. He stated the lie without a trace of guilt. If that was what it took to flush the truth out of this murderous piece of trash, that was what he would do. "She's out having fun, living the life and you're here…" He shook his head. "For how long?"

Eric remained silent.

"You've been wronged. I can see that," Travis said.

"She started all this," Eric said unexpectedly as he shook his head. "She's the reason I'm here. It wasn't my fault."

He sat up straighter, drawing himself back, almost defensive.

"I believe you," Travis encouraged.

"Do you?" he said with the original sulky edge that had lessened slightly as if he were feeling slightly more talkative. "She always said we'd be together forever, that she'd never leave me. And now I'm here and…" His face shut down, as if he knew that he'd said too much. He shoved back from the table.

"Eric," Travis began. "I can help you." In the back of his mind he could only thank whatever stars had aligned that Eric hadn't demanded a lawyer be present. It was a possibility that might have deep-sixed this idea before it had even begun.

"Help me what?" he snarled. "I'm going to die in this hole and you know it."

"You help me, and I can help you," he said. "If you're sentenced…"

"I don't need your help," he gritted through clenched teeth. Spittle fell on the table. "It's over. I don't need you or any of your twisted promises." He stood up in a rush and the chair clattered backward. Behind him the door swung open. Before either of them could move farther, the guard was in the room. In seconds, he'd grabbed onto him.

Eric's eyes met his.

It wasn't the first time he'd faced evil and it wouldn't be the last. Still, he was glad to walk out the gates of the prison and leave Eric Solomon far behind.

The trip hadn't been as successful as he'd hoped. He'd proven only one thing. He had confirmation from the killer himself that he hadn't acted alone. More amazingly, he'd also had confirmation that the other killer was female. But whether Eric would ever admit to that in court was another matter. They'd work on that when the time came. Most important, he knew that he needed to get Kiera into a safe house and they needed to do it faster than James had thought. They needed one now.

Travis was on the phone to James before he hit the road. He explained the situation and an hour later he was heading back to Cheyenne with orders to get Kiera packed and ready for her new life. He wasn't sure how that would go over. What he did know was that there was an APB out on a woman who might be the second serial killer. A woman who might have only one goal in mind, making sure that her last victim died.

This time the little over two-hour drive that stretched out in front of him felt endless. As he left Rawlins's city limits behind, he'd never felt more determined in his life. It was during the drive that he was able to contemplate, really think about how much Kiera had come to mean to him.

Even after this short time, he couldn't imagine his life without her. Despite that, he knew they were too different, their lives too disparate to ever pursue a relationship. He didn't know from one moment to the next where he might be or what he might be assigned to. And Kiera, she had her job, her love of her elderly patients and her passion for helping. He knew all that despite the little time he'd spent with her and he wanted so much more. He was blindly falling for her without knowing her like he should. And he didn't know if she felt the same way or not. It was too early in the game and yet his mother had always said that it had been that way with his father. It had been that way with two aunts and uncles as well—it was the way his family worked. They were romantics. He pushed his what-ifs aside and only hoped that she'd give him the chance to get to know her, a chance outside the boundaries of this case.

It was when he was on the last leg home with fifteen minutes to go that he heard the news that made fear run through him like it never had before, even when he'd faced off against the most dangerous criminals. There'd been an attempted prison break at the Rawlins state prison. No further details were released.

"Damn it!" He slapped the steering wheel. He was still too far away. He ordered Siri to give James a call. She answered back in her usual precise tones with a hint of an electronic accent and told him that Jane wasn't in his directory. He smacked his palm against the steering wheel again in frustration but gave the order again, this time slowing his voice down, and he had much better luck.

"No word yet on what happened," James said. "I believe it was stopped in time."

Believe wasn't a word that gave him any comfort. Had the break been stopped? One name ran through his mind.

Eric Solomon.

Chapter Sixteen

Travis pulled into the FBI office in Cheyenne at exactly one o'clock in the afternoon. The journey between Rawlins and Cheyenne had seemed to last forever. Only five minutes ago, he'd spoken to Reece, the marshal taking the current shift with Kiera. Reece had assured him that everything was well, there was nothing out of the ordinary. Considering all that had happened in the recent past, he'd drawn in a relieved breath at the news. Reece, not unlike Devon, was good. Travis was surrounded by good men, the best. Only last year, Reece had been instrumental in taking down a terrorist group. He could rely on any number of colleagues, but Reece Blackburn, like Devon, stood out. Assured by the call, he headed for the FBI office to report what had occurred with his visit to Eric. Thirty minutes later, inside the FBI building, he bypassed the elevator, for even a minute wait would have been intolerable, and took the stairs two at a time.

But the physical exercise didn't take the anxiety away. He didn't want to be here. He didn't want to be away from Kiera another minute. But there was no choice. There were things that needed to be done and things that he needed to speak to James about. They were specifics that needed to be put in place, and a plan that had to be put in motion to keep Kiera safe.

"James," he said as he stood in the doorway.

James nodded but his eyes remained on the laptop.

Travis took a seat as James contemplated the screen before looking up.

Travis told James the details of what had happened.

"Interesting," James said thoughtfully. He looked at the file on his laptop. "So, here's the new arrangement effective almost immediately. A safe house in Denver. Memorize the address and I'll be in touch," he said. "With the new information, well, this isn't a safe situation. Especially with the admission from Solomon. You and Kiera are officially a couple until this is over. Unfortunately, the place won't be ready until tomorrow morning. I'd suggest a hotel room in Denver. Have her use your last name, pose as a married couple. Maybe flip to her second name for good measure. I don't think you need any more than that— at least for now."

"Thanks, man," he said. "For getting this done so quickly."

James nodded. "Good luck," he said. But the look he gave him held something else that looked suspiciously like regret.

Travis didn't have time to consider what any of that might mean. He wasted no time in getting out of the office and heading to where he needed to be—with

Kiera. No matter how good Reece was, he needed to be there by her side.

Fifteen minutes later and two blocks from Kiera's house and it seemed like the distance between the FBI office and her home had increased dramatically. It was taking forever to get there. His mind was awash with thoughts, with what needed to be done.

It was two o'clock in the afternoon. He promised himself that he'd have Kiera away from here and on the road by three.

But minutes after Reece had left Kiera's condo, Travis walked over to Kiera and sat down on the sofa beside her. It was time to lay out for her the drastic shift in plans. It wasn't a job he relished for he didn't know how she would take it. He wasn't sure if she would cooperate and if she didn't, he didn't know if he could convince her to change her mind.

There was no way to preface this, so he met it head-on. "Kiera, it's not safe for you here."

She frowned, her eyes narrowing. "I don't like where this is going." She looked him in the eye as she stroked Lucy and the cat purred. "This is our home. I…"

He looked down. Damn, he hadn't thought about the cat or factored in its importance to her. An error right out of the gate wasn't good.

"After what happened, Kiera, we can't take the chance that it might happen again. We have to move to a safe house."

"What do you mean?" she asked. "You and the other marshals are protecting me until the trial. I'm safe."

"You weren't safe yesterday afternoon."

"But I'm safe now," she insisted. "You make me safe."

He met the look in her eyes, saw apprehension and something else—fear. He took her hands in both of his, ignored the cat and pulled her close. The cat me-owed. The damn cat could complain all she wanted, he thought. His lips brushed Kiera's and then he was pulling her against him. He kissed her deeper as her soft yet firm figure pressed against him. And he only wanted her closer, tighter.

When he let her go, she gave him a befuddled look.

"I'm starting work next Monday," she said after more than a minute had passed, as if that somehow changed what had happened. She shifted a few inches away from him, her lips still heightened in color, prettily blushed from his kiss.

"They're expecting me. They need me." It was as if she believed he would argue and she had her defenses in place.

She wasn't wrong. It wouldn't happen, it couldn't.

"Kiera, you can't stay here. They can get a temp in—I've already spoken to your supervisor."

"You what?" her voice went up in volume. "How dare you." She stood up. "I can't— I don't need..." She shook her head as if there were no words to say how upset she was. She walked a few feet away, her back to him. What was clear was that she was dodging the idea of a move altogether.

He followed her. He put his hands on her shoulders. He turned her around to look at him. No matter what she thought—this was happening. He wasn't taking any chances, not with her life—ever.

Her eyes never left his. They sparked with passion, with denial and with all the life he loved so much about her.

"You had no right."

"I'm responsible for your life," he said. It was true, for it was what it all came down to.

"You're nothing more than a bodyguard," she said as if downplaying his work might help her win the argument. "And I don't need one. I'm fine on my own. I'm armed." She looked over her shoulder and he followed her gaze to where the vintage Colt .45 sat on the coffee table.

"You didn't think so yesterday or the day before that," he said with strained patience. There were other arguments he could draw on like where and where she could not take the gun. All he wanted to do was check the time and hit the road. He drew on every ounce of patience he had. "What's changed? I've got that you have the gun, but don't think I don't know how you feel about using it. Odds are you couldn't shoot anyone if you tried. In fact, the last time around you scared the intruder off but I'm guessing that wasn't what you meant to do."

She looked at him with denial in her eyes.

He leaned over and kissed her again. And in the seconds after that kiss, everything changed between them.

Her upper lip quirked in the suggestion of a smile. "I could hear my aunt's voice telling me to crease their ear. Except, I was afraid. Afraid that I'd miss, kill her and you. So, I shot high." She didn't look at him. "I could have creased her ear. I've been to the shooting range. Months ago…" Her voice trailed off.

He guessed that she was realizing that a little practice did not make perfect.

"And work isn't an option," he said arguing a point that was in his mind, moot. He had a bigger issue to deal with but first he had to steer her from this one. "You'd endanger the residents of the care home."

She looked at him with tears in her eyes. She unfolded her arms. "Alright," she said. "I won't go back to work, not yet."

"Agreed. Not until I catch this piece of sludge and put them behind bars." The truth was, he was ready to put her over his shoulder and take her out of here kicking and screaming. But that wouldn't work. He needed her buy-in and he needed it quickly.

"Just because our security team claims that there have been no early morning calls doesn't mean that it's over. In fact—"

"It could mean something worse," she murmured.

"It already has meant worse," he said. "You were stalked and I was attacked."

They had little time. They needed to get packed and get on the road. Even with a drive that was under two hours, barring traffic, they needed to leave as quickly as possible. As it was, they'd be hitting rush-hour traffic in Denver. There was no getting around that. The traffic rush began now and would last well through the supper hour. Still, he wanted to get on the road and put distance between her and the danger that he now knew lurked here. But he couldn't push her and risk any opposition. He waffled about which approach would be best.

She didn't say anything. Instead she fell back down onto her sofa as if every bone and muscle in her body had turned to jelly.

"You've got to leave, with me, Kiera. To a safe house. You and me."

"Why? What's changed?"

"I went to Rawlins, to the federal jail."

A hand went to her mouth. "You saw him."

"I did. And he confirmed what we'd already come to believe, that there were two people that night and only one of them is in jail."

"And I'm the only witness," she said in a whisper and sank down onto the edge of the couch.

"Exactly," he said. "I'll tell you all of it on the road." He sat down beside her.

"We're that pushed for time?"

"I want us on the road by three at the outside," he said. "You're okay?"

She nodded. And he could see in her eyes and the set of her lips that they were finally on the same page.

"The safe house won't be set up until tomorrow but the important thing is that we're out of here, out of Cheyenne."

"I hate this," she muttered. "There's no other way?"

"No other way," he confirmed in a low voice that only emphasized the situation. He was pleasantly surprised at her reaction, by the lack of pushback from her. After her reaction about her job, he'd only assumed the worst.

"Okay," she said and stood up. "I'll get packed."

"Just like that?" he asked. He couldn't predict her.

"There's no choice is there? I mean, the only thing that seems to have stopped are the phone calls."

She was right there. According to Serene there'd been no calls since the third morning she was home. There'd been a dead-end on traces. In the meantime, he'd obtained a pre-paid phone for Kiera.

"No choice," he agreed. "And it's a hotel for us tonight," he said. "I'll tell you—"

She held up her hand. "I'm not ready to hear what he said. I..." Her voice shook. "Give me time on that. I need to know. I just don't... It gives me the chills, like I was there in that closet all over again."

"I get it. You'll ask in your own good time."

"I will," she said with a smile. "And probably sooner than you think. In the meantime, what else aren't you telling me?"

"One other thing." He hesitated to say it, unsure of how she was going to react. There was a split-second hesitation "We're going to be married for a while."

"Alright," she replied.

"Then we're good to go," he said, as if the cavalier words could make up for his shock at her easy acceptance of the new situation. They were heading into the unknown. He'd expected reluctance, fear even. And he was relieved that she reacted with none of that.

His phone rang. He looked at it and at Kiera. "I have to take this," he said.

She nodded as he stood up and went to the front door. He hit Answer as he opened the door and went outside.

It was James.

"You ready to head out?"

"Twenty minutes out," he replied. He didn't mention that he had yet to convince Kiera that this was the only way to keep her safe. "I'll message you when I'm there."

"Have you rolled out the situation for her?"

"She's aware we're going to a safe house."

"So. You have told her that she's going to be your wife for a while? Possibly gotten her agreement?" James chuckled as if already anticipating her response.

"The laughs on you," he said with a smile. "She knows and it's not an issue."

Travis disconnected seconds later and went back into the condo. He didn't look forward to what he only saw as long and anxious hours ahead.

Chapter Seventeen

They'd been on the road for thirty minutes. The prairie rolled out on either side of them, as the distant mountains rose in the background. He glanced over at Kiera. Anytime he had in the past, like now, it seemed that her eyes hadn't left the road. It was as if they needed to be there, as if she were the one driving. He sensed her tension. He knew leaving her home, her job and her life in Cheyenne wasn't easy for her. He also knew that the move was the safest option.

The cat meowed for the first time since the trip began. He had to admit that despite his reservations, so far, the animal had been no trouble.

"Lucy," Kiera said as she turned to slip her fingers through the wire front of the carrier. "Not that long and we'll be there. Promise."

She spoke as if the cat understood. He'd heard that this was a trait of many pet owners. Her bond with the animal was like a foreign language to him. He'd never had a pet. Neither his lifestyle nor his personality left him open to the idea.

"You're quiet," he said as another mile passed. He

glanced over at her, hoping if nothing else to start a conversation on how she was feeling, on how this impacted her. Anything would be preferable to the silence.

"I'm completely stressed by this. Leaving my home, leaving everything I treasure behind." She shook her head. "It's impossible to process. It's all been so much, too much."

She was silent for a minute.

He didn't say anything. He couldn't imagine all she'd been through and all she still needed to do to finally put this behind her. She was right, it was too much, and yet more kept being asked of her. There was no choice. But he admired the fact that with little complaint, she shouldered it all.

Minutes passed. He could feel her eyes on him. He glanced over. The late afternoon sun highlighted her high cheekbones, her natural beauty evident even without a trace of makeup.

"I hate that this is happening," she said after silence had again become heavy, uncomfortable between them.

"It's not forever," he promised. "After the trial, or maybe sooner, you'll be able to go home. One day, it will be as if none of this ever happened," he said. He wasn't sure if that would ever be the case. But she needed something to look forward to. She needed the silver lining, not the dark cloud that she'd so recently escaped.

"One day," she said in a quiet voice. She turned to watch a herd of elk in the distance, as if the sight would bring that normalcy into her life, as if it might bring it sooner.

So far, it had been an easy drive. But Wyoming was like that, miles of straight, uncongested roads. With a small population, traffic jams didn't exist. It was one of the things he loved about the state. Of course, there was more to it than that. He could also add the mountains, the wildlife and the raw, untouched prairie. All those things were reasons that he'd jumped at the chance when a position had come up here. The bonus, of course, had been the fact that this was the state where he had grown up and where the majority of his family still lived.

Minutes and miles passed. The scenery hadn't changed, only another herd of elk and a lone deer provided any change from the miles of prairie. They traveled in silence for a few miles.

"It will never be the same will it?" she asked as they neared the Colorado border. "My life, I mean."

He didn't know what to say. He guessed that what she had said wasn't really a question.

A minute passed and then two.

"You didn't believe there were two people who took me, did you? Even after calls and the threat," she said.

"That's not exactly true," he said glancing at her. "After the phone threats I still had doubts. But I was considering what you said and pushing to investigate the possibility. Then, after I was attacked..." He glanced at her. "If I'd known you better, I would have believed sooner. I'm sorry, you were right."

"Sometimes I think none of it was real, that it was just one horrifying hallucination."

"Right," he replied. "And that's the problem."

"You need evidence," she said.

"Exactly. Without it, you have us in a corner. As a marshal, it's my job not to take everything at face value. I'm obliged to question." He glanced at her. "There aren't any lawyers now. He's refused representation. But I can see that changing. Eventually he'll come to his senses. The lawyers will be worse—you realize that?"

Worse was an understatement. The defendant's attorney, should he acquire one, could literally tear her apart.

"I know," she said softly and yet with an edge in her voice. "Don't worry. Whatever happens, I'll survive," she promised.

He knew that she'd survived a lot in her life. Her mother had died when she was three. She'd never known her father. Her mother had been a single parent. What Kiera knew was that her father had been too young and too uninterested. He'd never offered support and declared he wanted nothing to do with her. Her parents had parted ways shortly after her mother learned she was pregnant. For Kiera it had never been a big deal. Even after losing her mother, she'd never thought to find the man who had fathered her. She had no interest and claimed she never would. Her aunt had raised her after that but had died only a half dozen years ago. As much as Travis cared about his aunts and uncles, he wasn't sure what it would be like to lose your only family member, the aunt who raised you. He knew that her aunt had no children and he could only think how lonely that would be with no siblings, no raucous family gatherings. It seemed odd to him.

"Like you survived your childhood?"

"No!" There was a note of surprise in her voice. "It wasn't like that. My childhood wasn't anything that needed surviving. Not at all. Aunt Nan was wonderful. Besides, I was so young when my mother died that I only have a few memories. Good ones but nothing traumatic. It was Aunt Nan's passing that killed me. I was eighteen. And after that, it was just me.

"What about you?" she asked.

He smiled, for he realized that in the time he'd spent with her it had been more him grilling her, and, of course, he had the advantage of having a file on her.

"Three brothers, a sister, my mom and dad, grandparents and a herd of cousins, aunts and uncles... Some days the list seems endless."

"Do you stay in touch with them?"

He smiled. "All the time," he said. "But it's more like they stay in touch with me." He thought how spoiled he really was and how little effort he had to put in to keep in touch. They did, as his mother would call it, all the heavy lifting. But once a year he had his grilling extravaganza for the entire clan. There was no set date due to his job and the unpredictability of his assignments. But it was tradition. And, on the first good weather weekend that he was home, he fired up the grill for the event. It was an event that he planned at least a week in advance.

"You're lucky," she replied and there was a wistful tone to her voice. "I'm betting you had fun growing up," she said. "Lots of baseball games?"

"A sport that I don't excel at," he admitted.

"What were you good at?"

"Golf," he said. "Not the sport to win the girls over, so I migrated to football in high school."

"Golf," she repeated. "If it makes you feel any better, Aunt Nan was an older mother and her idea of sports was bowling. I actually can still bowl a fairly good game."

The conversation stayed for a few minutes on safe ground, exploring the worlds of their childhoods before lapsing again into silence.

Ten minutes passed, then fifteen. The scenery was changing. They were getting close to the state border. She shifted in her seat as if she were ready to get out, stretch her legs and end this road trip.

The mountains were drifting farther back. The road felt less closed in.

"Okay, tell me, what did the creep say when you went to see him? Tell me what you can," she said. Her voice was soft and yet no less commanding.

"He basically said that he wasn't acting alone. And he confirmed that he had a partner and that she's female."

"What the lowly witness had already told them," she said with a hint of an edge in her voice. She looked at him. "Was it you who suggested that I be moved?"

"Pretty much. Although…" He didn't finish. He wasn't sure if he wanted to finish.

"Although?" she repeated. "That leads me to believe there's more."

There's always more, Travis thought. "It wasn't an easy decision to be made all around. But once the evidence of a second killer became a real possibility, once a stalker entered the picture, there's no way that we could do anything else but get you immediately to a safe place." His eyes were focused solely on the road for it was moving into prime time for deer and antelope to be crossing the highway. The animals were in grazing mode and not adverse to running, without warning, across the highway.

There was silence again for a few minutes as the late-afternoon sun danced across the prairie and the mountains retreated farther into the background. They crossed the Colorado border and the traffic slowly began to pick up. Time passed and soon they were no longer in laid-back, wide-open country. The uninhabited prairie slowly morphed into towns and then cities and eventually the urban and commercial sprawl that spread tentacles along the highway and led to the metropolis of Denver.

"How long?" she asked with a quiver in her voice. "How long before I can go home?"

His eyes were on the road. But the truth was he didn't want to look at her. He couldn't stand tears. He didn't know what to do. It wasn't as if he could hug her or even just make it better with words. He was driving. He had to stay focused and there was really no time limit he could give her. *Until it's over* wasn't the answer she wanted to hear.

He could feel her eyes on him. He knew that she wouldn't let go of the question. She'd wait patiently.

"It will be alright. We'll get you home, hopefully soon."

"I hope so," she whispered.

And, in the silence, he vowed that he would keep the promise of getting her home soon.

It was a promise he didn't know how he was going to keep.

Chapter Eighteen

They'd been on the road since midafternoon and the trip was close to over. It was almost five o'clock—the worst time to be hitting the outskirts of Denver. He looked over at Kiera. She was quiet as if caught in her own thoughts.

She glanced at him. "You okay?"

"Why do you ask?"

"You've been driving the whole way and it's crazy busy."

"Denver in rush hour. You've never been here?"

"No." She shook her head. "There wasn't money for trips, not after Aunt Nan died, and even before. We had to follow a fairly tight budget."

He imagined what she must make of seeing the urban sprawl that was Denver. The endless box stores as they neared the city, the vehicles that were bumper-to-bumper, the hectic pace of a large city so different from Cheyenne.

He gave her a glance and a quick smile. Not that he didn't enjoy his visits to Denver, not that it wasn't a beautiful city but the urban sprawl that led into it was only another reminder of why he loved the wide-open spaces of Wyoming.

"I'm beginning to appreciate Cheyenne," Kiera said as if she had read his thoughts. "This is too busy for me."

He kept his eyes on the road. But he couldn't agree with her more. Denver was an attractive city, but Cheyenne was the perfect size, at least for him.

They'd passed a number of hotel and motel advertisements. He'd already pinpointed a hotel a mile from where they were. It would be a relief to get off the road.

"I found a hotel close to the house we'll be moving to tomorrow."

"Alright," she replied. "I'm assuming you're checking in."

"I am," he said. With her having no ID, he would complete the registration at the hotel. His name was on no one's radar and using his name, acting as a couple, was part of the plan. Five minutes later he was taking their bags to their room.

"Are you hungry?" he asked. It was close to suppertime and he hadn't eaten since breakfast. He wasn't sure about her.

"Starved," she replied.

Guilt ran through him that he hadn't stopped and grabbed snacks for them while they'd been on the road. "There's a restaurant beside the hotel."

"Let's go," she said as she headed to the door. He guessed when she said she was hungry, she'd meant it.

"You said you grew up in Wyoming, or did I get

that wrong?" she asked fifteen minutes later. They'd been seated at a table in a restaurant that also had a large bar, where televisions were set up overhead for prime sports viewing. They placed their orders before getting back to the conversation.

"Except for a brief time in North Dakota."

"What was that like?"

He didn't want to tell her a single thing. They'd already spoken of their childhoods and while there was a lot more that could be said, he'd said enough for now. He only wanted to look at her. He was fascinated by everything about her. From how she picked up her napkin and rearranged it so that her cutlery was neatly laid over it, to how she seemed to take everything in—enjoying it all, despite their reasons for being here, despite the trip to get here.

Their food arrived and they chatted amicably, like friends, clearly skirting all the reasons they were in Denver. It was a nice break.

An hour later they were back at their hotel room. He held the door open for her and she walked by leaving a light scent of cinnamon behind her. He followed and tried to keep his eyes off the easy swing of her body. Her arms were well-toned, and he guessed that was a result of working out. It was something else they had in common. His job dictated that he be fit but truthfully, he'd work out despite it. The gym was a place that invigorated him, and a week didn't go by without at least two visits to it.

In their room, she looked at her watch. "It's only eight o'clock. Do you want to watch a movie?"

"Sure," he replied. He'd sat down on the edge of the bed nearest the door and the cat immediately curled up in a ball on his lap. He wasn't sure how that had happened. Tentatively, he stroked the top of its head. The animal purred and cuddled closer to his belly.

"How did you end up with the cat?"

"Lucy? One of our new residents rescued her. Two months later she had a stroke and ended up in the care home. So, I took Lucy. It works out well. I can bring her to work occasionally and Margaret can see her pet."

"They don't allow animals?"

She shook her head. "Visiting is fine but not living there. Many of the residents love animals but can't take care of them. Having them visit is the next best thing. They bring in cats and dogs usually, but…" She smiled. "I've seen the occasional rabbit come in. As far as Margaret and Lucy, I bring her in at least once a week. It's not just Margaret who loves seeing her. She brings so many smiles. You can't imagine." She took Lucy from him and plunked down on one of two queen-size beds closest to the window. The cat batted her chin and she chuckled. "Margaret and Lucy are handling the arrangement fine and I think Lucy has truly settled in."

She put the cat down. "We need snacks," she said, changing the subject. "For the movie," she finished when he didn't answer. "Should I go and get…"

"No," he said abruptly and knew from the way that

the smile had left her lips, that he had been too harsh. "I'm sorry. I meant that I will get them."

Five minutes later he was back with drinks, chips and a chocolate bar to share. She'd admitted earlier that she loved chocolate but couldn't eat a whole bar. She found it too sweet.

"To share," he said when he saw her frown at the bar.

"You remembered," she said, and the frown was replaced by a smile.

He settled down on the bed closest to the door. The movie was a comedy. She'd picked it and it was perfect considering the state of her life. They laughed and shared the junk food. It was strange for he felt like they were a team as darkness collected outside.

The credits were rolling when he turned off the television.

Kiera had yawned numerous times in the last hour.

"Time for bed," he said. The words were more of a fact than a question. It had been a long day for both of them.

She nodded. "Definitely."

She'd already claimed the bed nearest the window and that suited him perfectly. They were on the fifth floor—there was no chance of danger coming from the window. He preferred to be closest to the door. In case of intrusion or disaster, that was both the danger point and the escape route. It was easier for him to ensure her safety if he had control of the exit.

Fifteen minutes later, she was sleeping, and Travis was staring at the ceiling. Knowing she was a few feet away only awakened desires that he was struggling to keep under control. A shared room had been a bad idea. He'd be glad to be settled in the safe house and put some space between them.

He closed his eyes. But it was impossible to sleep. He wondered how long they would have to keep her hidden. He hoped that it would be a short time. He hoped that they could catch the killer soon. But he knew the odds were slim. They had no new intelligence. They had no idea who she was and only the assumption that the person who had attacked him was also a serial killer. If that was the case, they had Kiera's sketchy description to go on. James had indicated that based on his interview, the FBI would interrogate Eric again. But he had his doubts on whether the killer would give any more information.

An hour later, he was dozing off when a scream woke him. He turned on the light. Kiera was thrashing around. Sweat gleamed on her skin.

"No," she said. "No, please." The covers twisted around her and her hair streamed over the pillow.

He got up and went over to her.

"Kiera."

"No!" She clawed at the covers.

He took her hands in his. She didn't wake up, but the touch seemed to calm her. She stopped struggling.

Lucy mewed from her carrier.

"Travis," Kiera murmured but her eyes didn't open.

"I'm here, sweetheart," he said and lay down on the bed beside her. He didn't know if she heard him, for she wasn't awake. He put an arm around her and she snuggled close to him. Finally, she settled and seemed to go into a deeper sleep. He lay there as seconds ticked into minutes. The cat mewed again. He dropped one hand down and stuck a finger into the carrier, stroking the soft fur. The mewing stopped. The cat purred and then dropped into silence. Finally, he reached over and turned off the bedside lamp. Both Kiera and her cat were asleep as he lay awake listening in the darkness. With Kiera warm and trusting in his arms, he knew that his life had just drastically and irrevocably changed. For the first time in his life, he'd given his heart away.

OVER BREAKFAST, as they wasted time until the safe house would be ready at ten o'clock, they bantered like they never had with each other before. He wasn't sure how they got there, but somehow or other, one of them had taken them back to stories of childhood. It was an easier conversation compared to others they had had. The intensity of the last week, the horror that she'd escaped—all of it was put aside as memories of bucolic childhoods and crazy kid antics drew them closer to each other. The stories had him appreciating the child who had made the strongest woman he knew. He wondered what her aunt had been like to have raised a woman like Kiera.

He'd learned that she'd been a video game fanatic as a ten-year-old. In turn he'd shared that, as a boy, he'd been a baseball addict, watching as many televised games as he could. Except, as he'd said earlier, what he'd been good at was golf. He'd even admitted to her that golf wasn't something the other kids admired, not like being the star pitcher or quarterback. So, he'd become competent at the sports the girls admired—baseball and football, but he'd never been the best player.

She'd smiled at that.

They'd exchanged stories—stupid childhood acts that now only made them laugh. While her childhood had been more difficult than his, it seemed her aunt had been dedicated to making it the best it could be.

"She was amazing," Kiera said softly. "Aunt Nan loved nothing better than having fun. I couldn't have asked for a better childhood." She laughed. "Did you ever make homemade ice pops?"

He smiled, enjoying this side of her. She could easily hop from one story to another. She wove laughter through her stories and asked him questions when he didn't immediately provide a story of his own.

"As a matter of fact, yes. With fruit juice."

She made a face. "Ours too. But at the time— they were good. I think my aunt thought they were healthy." She smiled. "Despite losing my mom, I can't complain about my childhood."

Silence followed after that.

When he thought of it later, he knew that it had been a strange conversation to have. Two adults drifting back into childhood memories not once but twice—he remembered the conversation on the road, passing the time as they got here—to this place, this time. Both conversations had served the sole purpose of taking them away for a few minutes from a situation that was too dire to contemplate. But the conversation also made him far too aware that there was little he didn't like about her. He just wished that it all boiled down to like. But he feared that it was building to more than that and he had nowhere to go, nowhere to run from an emotion that threatened to bring him to his knees.

He mentally pulled his emotions from the abyss. She depended on him to protect her. Seducing her, thinking of seducing her, none of that was part of the protection he was expected to offer. He needed to play this one by the book. And the book said no romance on an assignment. His intentions were good, but he made the mistake of looking at her, meeting her eyes. And he knew that whatever the rules were, she was in charge of the game. If she chose to break the rules, there was nothing he could do to stop her.

Chapter Nineteen

Later that morning, Travis pulled up to the low-rise beige apartment building where the safe house was located. It was one of eight apartment units in a lower-middle-class area that was built decades ago. It was the kind of area that was in need of a loving touch. It was a part of town that was occupied by people too busy making a living to give much consideration to looks. Or to notice strangers, thankfully.

"This is it?" Kiera asked but it was more statement than question.

He glanced over. She seemed tense, worried even.

He put a hand over both of hers.

"It will be alright," he said.

She looked at him. "It had better be, hadn't it?" She took in an audible breath before finishing her thought. "There isn't any other choice."

He squeezed her hand and let it go. There was nothing he could say that would change any of this. James had said that the apartment would be set up for them first thing in the morning and he'd confirmed that that was completed over an hour ago. Everything was ready to go. There was no room for doubt. This was the only choice they had to keep her safe.

Although, he thought that the FBI couldn't have picked a better area of the city. He realized that the choice was intentional. But, in his mind, he wanted the best for Kiera. Even in a situation like this. But this wasn't the best, not in comfort or status. What it was, was the best place to hide. It was in areas like this where nothing and no one seemed to stand out. It was the type of area that seemed to exist in every city. The housing was a jumble of beige and brown cheaply built mass housing units. It was a place in the city that had no real appeal. It was a place where it was easy to get lost, to disappear amidst neighbors only concerned with keeping their heads above water.

He unlocked the door to the second-floor apartment and ushered Kiera inside. She had a large bag and he carried another bag for the cat, along with the cat itself, in its carrier. He had a knapsack that he'd slung over his shoulder. He'd learned over the years to travel light. It didn't matter how long he'd be here, he could wash or buy more things if necessary.

He set Kiera's bags and the cat carrier down. He would let Kiera arrange the cat's things. He thought that putting her and her pet's things in place would help her feel more at home or at least settle in more quickly.

"I hope we won't be here for too long," she worried. "The shelter at home needs volunteers. We provide meals for disadvantaged and homeless. Come summer, many of the volunteers go on vacation. I usually give extra hours then." She looked up at him. "We won't be here that long, will we?"

"I hope not," he replied.

"Ann must be wondering where I am," she said, and he knew that she was referring to one of the seniors in the care home where she worked. "And Margaret, I hope she's not missing Lucy too much."

He didn't reply. She didn't seem to expect one as she walked away. He watched as she opened the fridge. He knew it would be well-stocked. That was standard in any situation like this.

"Lasagna sound good for supper?" she asked.

"Supper? How about lunch?"

She laughed. "Thinking ahead. There's lasagna in the fridge and a whole lot more—milk, cheese, some cold cuts and a stack of microwavable dinners." She opened a cupboard door and shut it. "And cereal and coffee too. We won't starve."

"I'll get some coffee started."

"Sounds good to me." She closed the fridge.

"This isn't a bad setup," she said a few minutes later. She'd scoured the place checking out each room. It didn't take her long. The place was small—five hundred square feet at most.

He glanced at his watch. It was eleven o'clock and his stomach rumbled.

"I'll make sandwiches later, for lunch. That is if they've left us any bread," he offered.

She didn't answer. He watched her, unable to drag his eyes away from hips that were more generous than one would expect with her small frame.

Despite that, in his mind, they were perfect. Everything about her was perfect.

SUSAN BERKER COULDN'T get the last victim out of her mind. Kiera Connell was the one who had changed everything. It was because of her that Eric was in jail. It was because of her that her best friend and lover had been taken from her. She needed to not only finish what they'd started, but to get revenge. She could have none of that unless she found their last victim. But she'd disappeared. There was no sign of her. She'd guessed that she was in witness protection and the odds of finding her were remote. But she wasn't ready to give up. Even though Kiera Connell was in the hands of a US marshal and he'd taken her underground, it wasn't over. A crumb, that was all she needed. She cruised the only thing that might give her that crumb, social media. For days there was nothing on Kiera's social media, but she hadn't given up and her patience had paid off. Only an hour ago she'd hacked her account to see a brief conversation Kiera had had with her supervisor. She'd included a picture of a cat, to be given to one of the residents. And in that picture was the answer to where the feds had her hidden.

"One of the stupidest moves you've ever made. Your heart won over your brain," Susan said and felt happiness bubble up within her for the first time since she'd lost Eric. This was finally going to end well. Not exactly as she planned. But she'd adapt, write her own ending rather than one imposed by the authorities.

She could hardly wait. She looked at her watch. Denver, Colorado, that was less than two hours away. She clutched the wheel of the old white camper van with both hands. They were hands that were suntanned from too much time on the road, too much time behind the wheel. But for the last few years, she'd driven coast-to-coast, stopping only for the excitement of the hunt and of the sex that followed. It was what she lived for, that and Eric.

Past tense and all because…

She'd kill her. She put her foot on the gas. The thought turned her on almost as much as sex. Almost.

She had all the time in the world and she wouldn't let this one go. Kiera reminded her too much of the first young woman she'd ever kidnapped. The irony of it was that her runaway victim had returned to Denver, the place where Susan had grown up. It was also the place she'd escaped from all those years ago. She still knew the city's secrets and she knew where to find the victim. No one could hide from her there. For Denver was where it had all begun and where, if things worked out like she hoped, it would all end.

Chapter Twenty

Travis heard water running in the bathroom.

She was in the shower—naked. Washing her thick dark hair—caressing her skin with soapy fingers…

The thought broke off with a huge effort on his part. He had to divorce himself from them, for they only created an imagined image. It was an image that took him to a place there was no recovery, no going back from. If he went to that place, he'd be turned on every time he looked at her. He wondered how much of this he could stand. He needed to keep his distance and yet there was no distance to be had. The safe house wasn't meant for two people. While it was the best that could be done on short notice, it wasn't the best for them. But it was all they had and if it was to keep her safe then he'd fight the attraction that had no place between them. For, he'd rather be here, fighting his own desires than fearing for her life in Cheyenne.

But thin walls did little to mute the steady beat of the water and the sound did nothing for his hyped imagination. He needed to get out of here, get away. But there was nowhere to go. He was here to keep her safe. He needed to be with her and he wanted to be with her. In the shower—naked.

He couldn't stand another minute. He went to the door and opened it, and then he remembered the damn cat. He closed the door. It didn't matter, the hallway was stuffy, and outside the night air was too warm anyway to cool him down at all.

There was no television in the apartment. They were definitely living bare bones, at least for the moment. With nothing to divert his thoughts he grabbed a travel magazine he'd shoved in his pack. When he had time, he loved to travel, especially places where he could hike or ski. Last year he'd been to the Swiss Alps and the year before that, the Canadian Rockies. He didn't have a trip planned yet but...

He pitched the magazine aside. It skidded across the worn wooden coffee table before stopping in a precarious hang at the edge. The magazine had done nothing to ease his mind. This assignment, this safe house, was going to be much more challenging than he'd ever imagined. Here, there was no avoiding each other. That hadn't mattered before. But it mattered now. His attraction to her had escalated to the point that, for him, there was no turning back. He wanted her in every way a man wants a woman. He couldn't go there. But the space was so incredibly small that there was little opportunity to avoid the attraction that was threatening to overwhelm him.

IF SHE'D BEEN a braver woman, Kiera would have turned the tap from hot to cold. But, despite growing

up in Wyoming, she hated the feeling of being cold.
All that aside, she wasn't sure if cold water would
have done anything for her unwanted feelings other
than make her damned uncomfortable. She wasn't
sure if it was because the last two years had been a
dry spell as far as romance was concerned, or he was
just that hot. But something about Travis had had her
falling for him the minute she'd laid eyes on him. She
wanted him like she hadn't wanted a man in a long
time, if ever. Her mind kept turning to inappropriate
thoughts. She wanted nothing more than to run her
hands along his skin, to feel the muscle that defined
a body that was as much eye candy as it was allur-
ing. But it wasn't that. It was him, his strength, the
way he looked at her, even the awkward way he'd
picked up Lucy. Uncomfortable, yet willing to put
himself out there. There was nothing about him that
she didn't like. The problem was that she feared that
it was more than like.

"Get it together," she muttered reaching for the soap.
She had to get rid of these thoughts, her feelings—her
need for him, her desire for him. But the feelings were
growing with every minute they spent together.

She tried to think of the practical, the place she
was in life. She tried to think of this apartment and
where she would be kept safe until the trial. It was
exactly like Travis had said. Here, she needed for
nothing. Everything had been provided. Everything
except a safe place where she could retreat from the
unrelenting attraction she felt for the man assigned to
protect her. She couldn't escape him. Somehow, she

had to learn to deal with that attraction. She didn't know how she'd survive days trapped with him in this small apartment. For it was different than when they'd been at her place. There she'd been distracted by the nightmare that she'd so recently escaped and the phone calls that had followed. There, she'd had a bit more space. But even then, she'd been aware of him.

Without danger distracting her at every turn there was nothing to stop her awareness of the man assigned to protect her. He was no longer safely in her driveway, making cameo appearances. Now he was front and center, and she wanted him.

"Damn it," she muttered as she rinsed conditioner from her hair and turned off the shower. Ordinarily, she loved time in the shower. She'd often spend extra minutes just letting the water wash over her. The water and the quiet time settled her mind on many occasions.

Not today.

Everything was too different. Her life was upside down and the only constant right now was Lucy.

Lucy. She hadn't taken care of her, hadn't thought of her except to release her from her carrier.

"Darn it," she muttered. What had she been thinking? But she knew what she'd been thinking, outrageous irresponsible thoughts that had no relevance here.

It was a relief to have the concern for her pet push away her inappropriate feelings for the man who was her protector. She hadn't put food out for her, nor had she unpacked the litter box. She'd been too caught up in her own needs, or more important, her need to escape her desire.

When she stepped out of the bathroom with her hair still damp and dressed in jogging pants and a sweatshirt she stopped and smiled. Lucy was standing over her bowl and eating; her water bowl was on her other side and to the right and in the far corner, she saw the litter box.

"I was going to put that in the bathroom, kind of out of sight," he said.

She looked at him with a smile. "Perfect."

Everything about him was perfect.

"Are you going to shower?" she asked.

"Not now," he replied. "I've only got part of the family fed." He laughed.

"Thank you, Travis," she said softly, taking in his sexier-than-hell physique and totally falling for his softer side. He was everything a man could be, everything she'd dreamed of and what every man, until now, had failed to be. His only downside was his damn job. Despite that, she looked at him with new appreciation and if it were possible, heightened attraction.

She wasn't sure when he'd closed the space between them. She only knew the moment when his hands were on her shoulders. The moment when heat streaked through her, seeming to curl in her belly and ignite her desire all over again as anticipation amped it all. She was pressed against him like he would never let her go. Her arms were around his neck and she didn't remember putting them there.

She was caught in the moment, in the feel of his lips on hers, on the need for more and deeper. Her body easily folded into his. But her lips didn't immediately react to his kiss, it was like her brain wouldn't turn off, wouldn't allow her body to do what it knew to do instinctively. For a second and then two, she didn't react. Her lips were stiff against his. This was what she'd wanted since the first day she'd met him and none of what was happening felt real. She'd frozen in place.

"I'm sorry," he said pulling away. "That should never have happened."

"Never be sorry." Her voice sounded strange even to her own ears. There was a husky edge to it. All she knew was that she wanted more and that, if necessary, she would make it happen. That had only been a teaser. She reached up, taking his face between her two outstretched hands. His eyes met hers in an erotic, almost hypnotic way, as if the dance she now led was hers alone.

"Never," she repeated against his lips and turned the kiss from tentative to one that couldn't be stopped.

"I've never met anyone like you," he whispered against her lips.

She didn't say anything. She wanted him now. She didn't want delays and talking meant delaying.

She knew in her heart that she wanted him with everything she had as she ran her hands down his back, feeling the defined lines of a body that was sculpted through hard work and many hours at the gym. Like the man, his body was defined by will and character. It took determination to maintain such a sculpted body and she appreciated every hour he'd worked and every inch of skin that he'd toned.

"Beautiful," she murmured.

He pulled back but didn't let her go. Instead he gave her a rather quirky, possibly self-deprecating smile. "That's a first."

"No one's ever told you that before?"

"It's you who's beautiful, sweetheart."

His hand skimmed her cheek as if reluctant to take it to the level to which she'd already led him. She felt the edge of disappointment when he turned the tables, taking their passionate game back a notch.

But the disappointment lasted only seconds before he made his intentions clear.

"Come," he said softly, taking her hand and leading her to the bedroom.

In the small bedroom, she again took the lead as she sank down onto the bed and pulled him with her. She was on her side, as she slipped her hand under his T-shirt, skimming the hard-toned flesh. He let her for a minute, maybe two—the time melted away.

"Kiera." He spoke her name in a way that was as provocative as his naked skin against her hand.

She pulled his shirt off and caught her breath. She'd known he had a beautiful body and that wasn't even one of the reasons she was here with him now. She'd also fallen for the spirit that shone so beautifully from him. He was perfection—toned and hard, golden tanned skin that reflected his active job with hours spent outdoors. Her breath caught as she ran her hand along his flesh, feeling the tingle of her palm and the tingles of anticipation that ran through her body. She wanted more.

He wasn't going to give her more. He stilled her hands in their erotic exploration.

Disappointment ran through her at the rejection and was soon masked by expectation as his hands began to run over her, making her hotter than she could stand.

"Travis…" She wanted to feel him, touch him. She wanted her skin against his.

"Let me," he said in a gravelly murmur.

He pulled her blouse over her head. The cool air gently wafting through the room seemed to kiss her skin and she shivered. But that was immediately followed by the warm, erotic touch of his lips on her neck. She shivered as the caress dipped to her shoulder.

His hand rode over her bra before he had it unfastened, as her attention was on discovering the definition of his chest, of the slim taper of his hips.

"Stop," she said and grabbed his fingers that had been caressing her breasts, kissing his fingertips. Then she sat up, turning around, her knees taking her weight as she straddled him and slipped his jeans down over his legs and off. His underwear followed.

But he hadn't stopped. He'd been making putty of her body while she was doing that. His caresses had her so hot that she could barely think.

She barely noticed as her bra fell away, she could hardly say when the rest of her clothes followed, for his fingers danced across her skin and sent sensations rising in a mercurial flood that was quickly reaching the point of unstoppable. She wanted him, and she wanted him now.

He kissed her, hot and passionately, his hand running over her body, gently squeezing her breast. Her arms were around his neck, her lips on his as her tongue danced against his.

Even the second when he slipped on the condom was a second too long. And when he entered her it felt as if she'd been waiting for this moment, this man, all of her life. It was where she wanted to be again, and again and again.

Later, in his arms it was as if she'd never been anywhere else, as if it had always only been the two of them. As if nothing had come before. And the nightmare, for now, had slipped away, masked by the warmth of his arms and the beating of his heart against hers. For now, it was just the two of them, made safe in a world of their own.

Chapter Twenty-One

Kiera looked at her watch. The watch felt foreign for she was used to her smartphone but she'd left that behind. She grimaced. It was only ten o'clock and felt like three. They'd been in Denver for four days and this morning began their fifth full day. The days were long but the nights… She smiled wistfully. The nights were like nothing she'd ever imagined. She felt hot just thinking of the positions they'd tried and the games they'd played. The nights made the days worthwhile.

An hour had passed since Travis had left. He'd gone for milk and bread—standard supplies for their small kitchen. She wondered if there was another reason for his supposed grocery run. For, despite how intimately she knew him, there were things about him that she didn't know at all, things he kept close to the vest. The tall, strong, silent type could be utterly frustrating.

He'd been gone too long. She felt edgy, out of sorts and she didn't know why. In his absence, she was realizing that his presence was part of the reason she felt safe. She paced the room, holding Lucy for as long as the cat would tolerate it. Minutes later, she set her down and the cat paced, obviously wanting to go out. She didn't blame her. Neither of them had been outside since they'd moved to Denver. She would have loved to put a harness and lead on the cat and take her for a walk. She smiled at the thought. Her neighbors in Cheyenne had laughed when they'd first seen her walk the cat. But she was a firm believer in the fact that a cat should be no more left to roam free than a dog. She was in the minority in that thinking.

"I'm sorry, Luce, not today."

The phone that Travis had picked up for her rang. New phone, different number and still her heart jumped at the sound. She answered on the first ring.

"Where've you been?"

"You're sounding jealous, sweetheart," he said with a laugh. "Did you think I was with someone else?"

"Oh, give it a rest," she said but the disdain was missing from her voice. Instead there was a smile and a small laugh. It felt like she'd known him forever.

"Meet me in the parking lot and I'll take you for lunch," Travis said. "I think you need a break from that shoebox we've been cooped up in. Maybe a burger."

"Sounds fantastic," she replied.

She hung up with a rush of happiness. Leaving the apartment, going outside, made her feel like they'd successfully left the danger behind. Soon, everything would be alright.

TRAVIS HAD TO SMILE as he disconnected. Kiera had sounded like a long-term girlfriend or a wife. She was playing her part well. Too well. It was hard for him to pretend, for it made the growing feelings he had for her feel justified. Except they were in a fake marriage, a made-up relationship. She was going by her middle name Jenna and using his last name, Johnson. Fake or not, somewhere along the way, the relationship had become, to a certain point, real. Never would he have thought that the victim of a brutal crime would be the woman he fell for. It was neither the time nor the place for a romantic relationship. Except he didn't know if he could turn it around or if he even wanted to. She was the woman in his bed, the woman he wanted in his life, and he couldn't see himself walking away from that. The passion he felt for her had been played out every night since they'd reached the safe house. There was no going back for him and he hoped for Kiera too.

He pushed the thoughts from his mind. He was two minutes away from the place that they now called home. It was the home that they would be living in for the next few months. He couldn't imagine where their relationship would go in that amount of time. It frightened him as nothing in his life ever had.

The parking lot was just behind their apartment building and shared with two other buildings in the area. He was just about to turn in when movement caught his eye. Someone was in the lot. That wasn't unusual. Even as he hoped it was Kiera, his gut screamed that something was wrong. His foot was on the brake, as he put the vehicle in Park. Then he saw her. She had her dark hair braided as she liked to do. She'd said it kept her long hair out of her face.

Kiera.

He smiled. He was looking forward to seeing her, even though it had only been a little over an hour since he'd left. The truth was that he never tired of her optimistic chatter.

Then something else caught his eye and dread locked in his gut. She wasn't alone. He opened the door and got out, closing it as softly as he could, his eyes never leaving the scene in front of him.

Something shifted. Now he had a clear view. He couldn't believe what he was seeing. She was struggling. Being held—against her will.

What the hell?

Kiera's hooded captor was half a foot taller than her. She was held with an arm around her neck. As the pair struggled, he could see a glint—the possibility that her attacker held a gun.

Anger boiled within him. He'd made a colossal error, thinking that she was safe. Now she was in danger because of that mistake, his mistake.

Dread raced through him.

He was moving closer, cautiously to keep his presence undetected. He was at the edge of the parking lot, hidden by shrubs. Her captor was holding her in a choke hold. She was in a position that ensured that at this distance, he couldn't get a clean shot without risking hitting Kiera. And, as he considered his options, she was being forced backward, farther away across the parking lot. He couldn't reach her in time. And he feared that if her attacker became aware of his presence and of his intent, they would as likely kill her as not. But, if she left the parking lot with her abductor, the outcome would more than likely be the same. There was no choice. He had to take her kidnapper out. But from here, he didn't have a clear shot.

He swore through clenched teeth. Despite the angry words, it was fear that raced through his veins. He wouldn't let this happen. He couldn't, not now when he'd found the woman he wanted to spend his life with, the woman he loved. Not now, when the life of the woman he loved was at stake. There was no way he could lose her now. It wasn't going to happen. Someone would die. His attention focused on her attacker. It wouldn't be Kiera.

But, despite the weapon in his hand, his assessment of the situation wasn't optimistic. He might have a shot if he could get closer. The weight of the Glock was unforgiving in his hand, reminding him of its success rate. Except here, he had no chance of an open shot. Unless of course he could get a head shot. The only way to free her was first to get closer and second, to get Kiera out of the way. He wasn't sure how he was going to accomplish either of those things without making his presence known.

And, as he was faced with a no-win situation and no other options, the unthinkable happened. Kiera was free. He'd seen her push back as if she might have driven an elbow into her captor. It didn't matter how it had happened. It was his opportunity. With no seconds to lose, he fired, giving his position away. But her captor twisted in time and bolted away, unscathed. A shot was fired at him, as they stopped for a second to turn and shoot. The shot was wild. Then the hooded assailant was running toward a vintage van, thirty feet behind her.

Kiera was nowhere in sight.

Panic flooded him as he ran toward the scene. Where the hell was Kiera? Had she been caught in the crossfire? He couldn't lose her, not now. He was running as if his life depended on it, except he was running toward danger. For Kiera's life depended on him. And, as the soles of his sneakers hit the pavement, life and death flashed before him as he ran faster than he ever had before.

Kiera.

She lay in a heap on the pavement, like a sack of potatoes that had been dropped and left. Whether she was injured or not, he didn't know. He only bent down long enough to put his fingers on her wrist and feel her pulse. It was steady. There was no more time. She was alive and he had a window of opportunity to end this—to stop the kidnapper.

But the scene had changed in mere seconds. It was like a kaleidoscope shifting without warning. The attacker was behind the wheel of an old van, which was very like one he remembered as a kid, a camping van. It was at least twenty years old. He was too late to get a clear shot. But he could cripple the van. Maybe slow them down by taking out a tire. And then, that option was taken off the table as the van spun around and took off in a squeal of tires as the sun glinted off the worn paint, the plate smeared with dirt and unreadable, as it sped out of the parking lot.

He fell to his knees beside Kiera. She was struggling to stand with a hand on the pavement steadying herself.

"Are you hurt?"

"No." Her voice broke. "Just scraped."

He saw the quiver of her body, realized how traumatized she was and took her in his arms. She was alive and that was all he had prayed for. Still, he had a sinking feeling that he was at war and the battle he'd lost was crucial to the victor's success. He shoved the thought aside.

"Damn it," he muttered, frustrated that her kidnapper had gotten away. They'd been so close. The van was out of sight; he could only call the attack in. Still, he was angry that he couldn't do more. The anger was muted only by the knowledge that Kiera was safe. He'd succeeded in saving the one thing that was important, the one person who mattered. Her arms were around his neck, her heart was beating against his chest. He held her as if he would hold her forever. And he would, except in this situation they needed to move. Whoever had attacked her had gotten too close. The safe house was compromised.

"You're sure?" he asked.

"Shaken," she said.

"Was the van in the parking lot when you arrived?"

"I'm not sure. I didn't see it. It was so sudden. I was grabbed from behind."

Her body shook even as he held her.

"I managed to get away from her. I didn't think I could. She's unbelievably strong," Kiera said in a trembling voice against his shoulder.

Admiration ran deep in him. She had more guts than almost anyone he knew. She was emotionally steady despite escaping possible death for the second time.

"Did you see them?"

"Her," she corrected. "And no. I didn't. She was behind me." She shuddered. "I knew that voice." Her own voice shook. "I remember it the night I was kidnapped."

Travis bit off the curse that didn't come close to tamping his frustration. If Kiera was right and if the theory of a second serial killer held, that meant that the killer had again proved herself far more resourceful and as a result, deadlier, than the one they had in custody. For, she'd not only found Kiera, but she'd flown completely under the authority's radar. Again.

"Are you alright?"

Kiera's voice was soft and full of concern, yet there was determination, a thread of steel running through it.

He looked at her with disbelieving admiration. Even now, she was thinking of someone else.

"I'm fine, Kiera," he said.

But, despite the unimaginable trauma she'd been through, it wasn't over. Whoever had attacked her had gotten too close. He didn't doubt that they wanted to finish what they'd started so many days ago. It was a more tangled web than they'd thought. And the key to that web had disappeared—again.

Chapter Twenty-Two

Travis held Kiera's hand as he began to scour the area where the attack had happened, and then where the van had been. In the meantime, he didn't plan to let her out of his sight. Yet, he needed to make a thorough examination of the area.

"Travis."

He looked at her quizzically.

"I'm not two," she said but there was no censure in her tone, only a resigned edge and a half smile.

"I know," he squeezed her hand. "Call me overcautious."

"I don't need to," she said with a shaky laugh. "That quality is pretty clear."

There was nothing to say to that. He had other thoughts, bigger thoughts on his mind, like finding out who the woman was who was terrorizing Kiera. How had she tracked them to the safe house?

He was on the phone to put in a brief report, notifying James and getting a search going on the van.

"What are you thinking?" she asked as he disconnected. "How she found me?"

"Yes. I have no answers. But I know one thing. The safe house is compromised. We'll have to move."

"I'm sorry."

He stopped. He'd expected her to be frightened, angry but not sorry.

"What do you mean you're sorry?" The words were quick. He had little time. He thought of cordoning off the area, but he had no time for that. He had a matter of minutes to examine the crime scene before someone arrived to get their car, park their car—who knew what—and contaminated the area. In the process, he also had to make sure that Kiera was safe. He was afraid. Afraid that he might lose her again. He'd never felt this way. In fact, it was like he was far more traumatized than she was—far more concerned. He needed physical contact, the heat of her skin against his to reassure him that she hadn't been kidnapped or worse. He needed to imprint her skin on his to remind him that she was alive and safe and where she needed to be, at his side. Or, more appropriately, make sure that she was where he needed her to be.

"Travis, I'm alright," she assured him. "You can let go of my hand."

"Okay," he agreed for all it took was her voice to make him realize that he was overdoing it. "Stay beside me."

"Alright but, Travis. I can identify her."

Sweet mother, he thought.

"This time I saw her face more clearly. The last time wasn't enough to recognize her in a crowd, except maybe by her hair but that's easily changed. This time was different."

Elation ran through him. They'd get a sketch artist and see what they could come up with. He'd reported the attempted kidnapping only seconds ago and the FBI's forensic response team would be sent out to gather any evidence. He didn't want to leave anything to the chance of it disappearing between now and when evidence could be gathered properly. He could see nothing but a dark oil stain where the van had parked. Then, he turned and saw a small white object standing out against the dark pavement.

He went over, bent down and picked up what appeared to be a keychain tag. He turned it over. And on second glance he knew that he was looking at another kind of tag, similar to his own, a gym fob. He looked at the lettering and saw the name—All Seasons Fitness.

Kiera was right behind him. He knew that instinctively. And then the warmth of her arm brushed against his.

"What do you have?" she asked in a voice that was calm despite what she'd just been through.

"I'm not sure," he replied as he looked at her and didn't bother to mask the admiration he felt. Attacked in a parking lot, almost kidnapped and she wasn't falling apart. Of course, he thought with regret, she'd been through so much worse. Yet it worried him that she seemed so okay now. That wasn't normal.

"It could be nothing or it could be everything. What I know for sure it that it's a gym fob and it was dropped very near where the van she escaped in was parked."

"You mean it might have belonged to the woman who tried to kidnap me." Her voice shook as she said the words. "It might be a way to track her?"

"It's a long shot but it could be a clue," he replied, relieved to hear the shake in her voice. Shaking nerves was a normal reaction for what she'd gone through. He put his arm over her shoulder drawing her close, trying to offer her some comfort, some assurance that she was safe. But he'd promised that once before and failed in his promise. He doubted he'd ever forgive himself for that.

"Are you alright?" Travis asked. He couldn't believe it had happened again, and on his watch. He'd thought she was safe, that she was secure. And instead, now their cover was blown.

"Do you really think that it was hers?" Kiera asked as she looked at the key fob. "Somehow, I can't imagine someone with such a sick bent doing something as normal as going to a gym."

"I agree," he said. "But I can't discount the possibility. And you'd be surprised. Many violent offenders keep relatively normal lives."

"A front," she said.

"Exactly."

"That could put an interesting aspect to her personality."

"How so?"

"Well, if it's the case, she's concerned about her

physical health and strength." She frowned and looked at him. "Am I right?"

"The hazards of her line of work," he said.

"And this might be a clue," she said looking at the fob.

There was a determined look in her eyes and he realized that she was never going to roll over and play the victim. She hadn't from the very beginning. No matter what happened she was willing to fight. He also knew that she wasn't going to do it alone. He was going to be by her side every step of the way.

He had to focus on what might be a crucial bit of evidence or nothing at all. The gym fob. It was the standard type used by most gyms to keep a record of their clients. It was used to gain entry, the bar code tracking the number of times a client appeared at the gym.

Five minutes later they were back at the apartment. She was sitting on the couch with a worried look on her face and he was punching in Serene's number.

She answered on the first ring.

"What's up?"

"Can you check a gym called All Seasons Fitness?"

"Sure. Can I ask why?" she asked.

At another time he would have found her question amusing. Now he only found it a time-consuming irritant. That aside, the question wasn't unexpected. Serene had always said that she'd love to do field work. Despite her abrupt, get-it-done manner, questions weren't unexpected. Her curiosity was boundless and sometimes he thought her talent might be wasted, confined as it was in the office.

"It's complicated," he said. "I found a key fob that may be connected to the case."

"Enough said," she responded in a voice that was still filled with curiosity.

"If you can, I need the closest gym. Also, can you give me their locations throughout Denver, if any, and if they have a presence in Wyoming. I need the exact location of the gym where this fob belongs and to who. I need that right away."

"On it," she replied. A minute later she had the specification of the gym for that key fob along with a string of other locations for the gym across the country. "One problem, I had a hard time getting any information on the account. The tag is scraped up and that's all the information I can glean from it. Nothing on the individual it might belong to."

With that resource exhausted, he disconnected from Serene and turned to Kiera. She was looking at him with interest. She'd been listening to his end of the conversation and had drawn her own conclusions. "You think there's a connection between this and the killer, to Cheyenne?"

"It's a long shot, Kiera. This might be nothing or…"

"It might be everything," she said in a soft voice that he had to strain to hear.

"I wouldn't say everything," he replied putting his arm around her shoulders. "In the meantime, are you up for a little detective work?" It was no question.

For if she said no, he wasn't sure what he was going to do. What he did know was that he couldn't leave her alone. Whoever was after her, they'd found her here. They knew she was in Denver. They'd been compromised. James was already getting them another safe house. In the meantime, he needed to keep her with him.

"You think it's not safe for me to remain alone?"

"Not here," he replied. "I'm going to the gym and you're coming along. I'm not taking any chances."

"Then I'm not taking any chances either," she said.

He frowned, puzzled at what that might mean until he saw her scoop up Lucy and put her in her carrier.

"You're kidding me?"

But he knew as soon as the words were out of his mouth, that she wasn't kidding, she was deadly serious. He could see that in the frown and the sparkle in her eye that told him she was determined. That nothing was stopping her.

"Until it's safe, she's coming with us."

The way she'd looked at him, the tone of her voice, it was enough for him to know that there was no point arguing, at least for now. He was only going to the gym, whose address Serene had given him, to ask a few questions. There was no way that the cat was a problem, an annoyance but nothing more than that. He could deal with the inconvenience, as long as he knew that Kiera was safe.

"Alright," he said as if there'd ever been a choice. And in that moment, he knew. He saw the love that she had to give—the empathy she had; he knew that when this assignment was over, he couldn't leave her. He was hers, if she'd have him.

SUSAN WAS CURSING under her breath. She'd failed. That was a fact she couldn't accept. She could accept it no more than she could accept the fact that Eric was in jail waiting to die. She knew that would be the outcome. There was solid evidence against him—she knew, she'd followed the case religiously.

She missed him. And she was angry that it had to be this way. But she knew that someone had to be held responsible and she'd given the authorities a fall guy for when her luck ran out. It had worked exactly as she'd planned. He'd been set up and there was not a stick of evidence that anyone else existed.

Until… She fisted one hand. Until they'd taken the last victim. If the victim hadn't escaped, all of this wouldn't have happened. Kiera had destroyed her family, destroyed her life. And for that, she deserved to die. Except, once she was dead their evidence wasn't so solid against Eric.

That didn't really matter. She was resigned to the fact that their partnership was over. It was getting stale anyway. She was ready for new blood. She passed a teenager on a bicycle. Someone like him, she thought. Not today. But one day she would go out trolling and find herself another teenager. One who she could raise, turn into a man who would make her not so much proud as satisfied.

That was all one could ask for in life.

She turned a corner. It was another mile to the

rental house she'd found so recently. Another alias, another strange house. It didn't matter. What mattered was tying up the loose ends and making sure that Kiera Connell died. But first she needed to take out her bodyguard so she could get to her. She thought of working out—she was always able to think at the gym. She belonged to a franchise where she could exercise pretty much in any city she was in. She scrounged through her bag. Her key fob was gone!

"Damn," she muttered. Mentally, she retraced her steps. The key had been in her pocket. Where had she dropped it? She needed to think.

She pulled into the driveway and stepped out. A ball rolled beside her.

"Hey, throw it back," a boy shouted.

She smiled. Her attention wasn't on him but on his companion. He'd be a looker when he grew up and soon she would need another project, another partner. The thought was fleeting as were the earlier ones. She picked up the ball and hurled it, hard and true. The move was unexpected, and it knocked the second boy off balance.

"Hey, you stupid…"

The expletive was lost on her. It didn't matter what he said. One day he would be nobody but somebody's tramp. It was what this neighborhood raised up. Sadly, he would not be hers. She had more important things to consider—closure first. She couldn't move forward without that and closure had just become much more difficult.

Chapter Twenty-Three

It was an hour before Travis and Kiera left what was no longer a safe house and headed to the location of the closest All Seasons Fitness. The route took them even farther from the city center than they already were. Here, there wasn't much as far as suburban development. And as they neared the gym, it became even more barren. They passed a tract of land that looked like it might be in the process of being developed. And farther on there were patches of neglected industrial lots. It wasn't a vibrant area and he wondered why the gym had picked this location. It was definitely on the fringes of Denver. The building that housed the gym was on the edges of a lot full of scrap metal and a run-down warehouse. On the other side he could see the start of a neighborhood of box stores. To the south there were low-cost apartments and assorted housing. It was an area ripe for developers to move in to claim land that was becoming more and more valuable.

The parking lot held a handful of cars. It looked like a location that might go belly-up soon, Travis thought.

"I'll wait here," Kiera said. "There's no point in me going in."

He wasn't so sure. Not that there was any danger and not that she wouldn't wait for him. He wasn't concerned for her safety, at least not here in this moment. Despite their speculation, the fob and this gym was a long shot. It could have been sitting in the parking lot for days and likely had been, considering its state. And, as far as this parking lot, despite the neglect of the surrounding area, it wasn't one known for a high crime rate. He still hated to leave her. But he knew that she was shaken by what had happened earlier and was more comfortable sitting in the vehicle than tagging after him. She'd said so. And here, there was nothing to cause concern. Her attacker was long gone. She was safe here and he wouldn't be gone longer than a few minutes.

She gave his hand a squeeze. "I'm fine."

"Alright," he agreed. "Keep your doors locked. You've got your phone?"

"Of course," she said with a smile.

"I won't be long."

"I'll keep Lucy company," she replied.

He nodded and wondered again how she could be so darn attached to the cat. In her situation a dog would have been better. And as far as he was concerned, no pet at all would be ideal. But it wasn't his life or his choice. He pushed the thoughts from his mind. He had other things to focus on.

He looked at the key fob. There was a good chance it had no connection with her kidnapper. He guessed that it had lain in the parking lot long before the attempted abduction. There was only an off chance that it could be the clue that turned everything on its head. Of course, he hoped for that, but he knew what the odds were. He dialed down his expectations every time he'd faced a situation like this. The hope that it was the clue that cracked the case was a long shot.

As he walked toward the entrance to the gym, a couple of young women left with bags slung over their shoulders. He stopped at the entrance and turned, watching as they got into a VW sedan and drove away. He glanced back at the SUV where Kiera sat; she caught his eye and gave him a wave.

She was fine. He was worrying unnecessarily. The attacker was long gone, that was a given. That aside, he just didn't like her out of his sight. Especially considering everything that had happened. He needed to learn to step away in the times that he could. This was one of those times. She was away from the compromised safe house; she was with him. She couldn't be any safer.

He went into the building. There, he made his way through a large area with benches and shoe racks and wound his way to the entrance on the main floor. He decided to give the fob the acid test and used it to swipe in. The buzzer sounded, freeing the gate. The young woman at the desk looked at him with a smile.

"Here for a workout?"

"No. Actually, I found this." He held out the fob.

"I see," she said. "And it let you in. Definitely belongs here, then."

She took the fob from him and ran it under the scanner. She looked at the screen and then back at him.

She frowned.

"What's wrong?"

"I'm not getting an account coming up," she said. "It's pretty banged up. I'll see if I can find something in the records."

A minute passed.

She typed some more, frowned and then pulled out a notebook from beneath the counter. She muttered as she scanned the entries and flipped a page. Finally, she looked up. "I'll make sure she gets it."

She.

That one word was like a glaring siren between them.

"Can you tell me the name, please? I'm Travis Johnson, United States Marshal." He pulled out his ID and showed it to her.

"Yes, of course. Susan Berker."

"Is there an address, phone number? Anything else—age?"

"An age—forty-two—but no address. Only a phone number." She gave him the number.

"Anything else?" he asked.

"No." She shook her head. A curl of black hair escaped one of the dozen or so braids that were held back with a purple-and-white headband.

"We don't collect data on our clients. That's all the information we have on any of them. Sorry."

"Did she have a locker here?"

"No. She didn't. And…" She looked at the computer. "She hasn't been here in a few days. I'm sorry I couldn't be of more help."

"Excuse me," a soft voice said behind him.

He turned around to face a young woman with soft, soulful eyes and a worried expression. "I heard you asking about Susan Berker. I may be able to help you."

"Do you know where she lives?" he asked hoping for the impossible.

"Yes," she said, much to his surprise.

"I was at her place on Friday." She blushed. "She took a liking to me. I've only seen her here twice. Anyway, Friday I watched her lift weights. She was amazingly fit." She paused. "When I was in the change room, she came over and asked me if I'd like to come to her place for…" She blushed. "You know."

Travis nodded. He did know. A sexual encounter, the details of which had no relevance to what he needed to find out.

"I said yes. But when I went to the address she gave me, she wasn't the same."

"What do you mean?"

"At first everything was okay. She gave me a hug and invited me in. Then she gave me a cup of tea. There was something off about the tea. I took a sip and couldn't drink any more. She kept pushing me to drink it."

That had Travis's attention. He guessed the tea was drugged. That put a whole new spin on what type of encounter this might have been turning into.

"Was she violent at all?"

"No." She frowned. "She wasn't happy with me when I didn't drink the tea. Then, she suggested that we play a game and brought out handcuffs. I saw the handle of a gun in her pocket and that kind of freaked me out. Everything was getting beyond weird. I told her I needed to use the washroom and slipped out her side door instead."

Minutes later, with the address entered on his smartwatch, Travis thanked her and watched as she headed to the change room. He stood to the left of the desk and mulled over what it all might mean. With answers only came new possibilities as old questions ran through his mind. How had the killer found Kiera? Was it possible they'd been tracked here and if so, how?

He contacted Serene. "Can you check if Kiera has been online since she was discharged from the hospital?" He knew that she'd been warned but he also knew of her soft heart.

Minutes later he had his answer. One interaction, one message to her boss and a picture. Her soft heart had left her vulnerable, again. Although she'd been warned to stay off social media, he guessed that she hadn't thought that one private message would be a problem. A picture of a beloved pet to remind an old woman that her cat was well cared for and safe was all that was needed. Her account had been hacked and her location traced. All it had taken was a little patience and a little tech savvy to pinpoint exactly where Kiera had gone.

KIERA LOOKED AT her watch. She was tired of waiting. It was a cool day; Lucy would be fine in the SUV for a few minutes. She unlocked the door and then she reached for the door handle. She was dying of curiosity to see if Travis had found something.

Her hand was still on the handle when the door was almost ripped open, and the handle flew out of her hands. The beginning of a scream died in her throat as she faced a wild-eyed middle-aged woman with wide gray streaks running through her long black hair. She knew her, was familiar with that face. But that was of little concern. What was, was the gun in one hand and the hate in her eyes. Or at least that's what she felt as her first instinctive reaction, that and a huge knot of fear.

"Get out!" the woman demanded in a throaty, hoarse voice that could be as much male as female. Except she was definitely female. Kiera recognized her from only three hours ago. She'd tried to abduct her once in a parking lot and somehow, despite Travis's precautions, she'd found them here. Now she had her arm and was yanking her out.

There was no time to consider any of that. Kiera fought desperately. She couldn't be taken again. For she knew the face and the voice. Her second kidnapper. Fear threatened to paralyze her, but she couldn't let it. Instead, she managed to pull away and tried to shimmy across the seat, toward the driver's seat.

"Get out!" the woman repeated. The grip on her arm was painfully tight. It was unbreakable. She was being yanked toward the door despite her efforts.

She could let it continue and land on her head on the pavement or do what the woman said. There was no choice; she held a gun and she held the advantage in strength and in spades.

Out of the corner of her eye she saw the entrance to the gym and hope breathed in her heart. But it was empty. Travis was nowhere in sight.

"Now!"

The woman pulled so hard that this time only a twist of her body kept her from falling headfirst onto the pavement. She scraped her knee and managed to right herself. The gun was hard in her back, reminding her of the fact that she had no choice.

"Move!" And as she took the first step toward the beat-up white van, she knew that it was over. The chance that she could escape twice, minimal, three times defied the law of—well, everything. She swallowed back the bitter taste of dread and prayed that Travis was as good as he claimed to be.

Chapter Twenty-Four

It was an ugly word and it exploded from Travis in a burst of horror and anger as he raced across the parking lot. He'd seen the struggle as he'd reached to open the door. Kiera was pushed into the driver's side of an old white van and a woman jumped in behind her. The van was taking off with a squeal of tires as he raced out of the building. He ran like he'd never run before. But it was futile. The van was out of the parking lot and speeding down a side road. His heart pounded. He couldn't believe that this had happened, again. Anger and disbelief raged through him. He'd failed. He flung open the door of his vehicle and faced the fact that she was gone. Only Kiera's cat peered at him from her carrier.

He started the SUV and had it in gear almost in one motion. He wouldn't let this happen to her, not twice in one day, not three times in a lifetime. He was peeling out of the parking lot after the van. The state of his tires and the amount of rubber he was leaving behind on the pavement was not a consideration. He couldn't believe that this could have happened again, that it was happening at all. The van was already out of sight as he left the parking lot in hot pursuit. They'd taken an intersecting road and disappeared. All he had now was the address the woman in the gym had given him. He had to hope that was where she was headed. It was all he had. He couldn't consider that he might have erroneous information.

The woman at the gym had indicated that it wasn't that far away. He put in a call to James and soon the FBI agent's voice filled the SUV.

"Wait for backup," James said. "I'm serious, Travis. The last thing you need to do is endanger yourself, as well."

"I'm sorry, James. I can't promise you that," he said as he disconnected the call. He let it ring after that. He had no further need to talk to James. James knew nothing that would help him; he had only demands that would hold him back from chasing the pair down. He knew James would get backup out. But he couldn't wait for anyone, not with Kiera again in the hands of a mad woman. Instead, he punched in the address on his GPS. Normally, he would have pulled over. Normally, he would have cared about distracted driving. The only thing that mattered was getting to Kiera in time to save her.

"Hang in there, Kiera," he muttered. He was speeding along a road that bordered an industrial section. That was the only bit of luck he'd had so far. He could speed without qualms in this area.

He couldn't lose her now. Not when he'd finally realized how much she'd come to mean to him. He took a corner so hard that the carrier slid across the seat and the cat let out a startled meow.

"Sorry," he muttered and didn't give a thought to the fact that he'd apologized to a cat. There was only one thing, one woman on his mind. He had to get to her in time. He had to stop this atrocity before it went any further.

The GPS had him at two miles away from his target. Two miles was nothing and yet it was everything. Within a minute he was in a residential area that seemed filled with worn, broken-down houses. He noticed a child's tricycle that looked like it was abandoned in the front yard, left to rust in the elements. Again, they were fleeting thoughts. He had to slow down—tricycles meant kids, families. His hands ached from a too-hard grip on the wheel. He was taking a chance. He didn't know if this was where they were headed. He only hoped he was right. If he was wrong, Kiera could be lost to him. He tried to push the thought from his mind. But the doubt kept returning and the dread of it made his stomach ache and his head pound with fear. The killer could be taking her anywhere. The address the woman had given him may or may not have been her home. It could be anything—belong to anyone.

The sprawl of Denver was unending. Even here, on the edges of industrial commerce, where the majority of the houses were neglected, a crane loomed in the distance. He was a few blocks away. He took another corner too fast, and this time he offered no apology when the cat's carrier slid again across the seat of the SUV.

Another block, the housing seemed even worse, more dilapidated, more neglected. Another kid's bicycle lay across the sidewalk like it was dropped and forgotten. A block ahead and three houses in, he stopped one house back from a worn brick bungalow. It was the kind built thirty years ago in a boom that had poor construction married to high demand and an influx of lower-middle-class workers. The house had seen better days. He turned off the engine. And, despite the urgency that was knotting his gut, he sat and took account of the situation. The white van was in the driveway. There was no one on the street. All was quiet which was good and also disconcerting. A door slammed, followed by a dog's bark.

His gun was out, kept to his side where it wasn't the first thing anyone might see of him. He closed the door in a controlled move, so the door clicked shut. Everything was silent. But they hadn't been there that long. They couldn't be. He was only minutes behind them.

He moved cautiously, bent over as he went up the drive on the side of the van farthest from the house. He peered in a window of the vehicle. Nothing. As he already guessed, the van was empty. A crumpled sweater lay on the backseat and a potato chip wrapper was on the floor. Otherwise there was no dirt or dust. It looked like it had been recently cleaned.

He wondered at that. Despite the van's age and environment, it had been kept meticulously clean.

His answer was only speculation and something he pushed to the back of his thoughts. But, if she was continuing their murderous spree, even without her partner, then this was probably the vehicle she was doing it in. And cleaning up any evidence as she went. He didn't take his mind to the darker place of what that evidence might be.

He rounded the van, keeping low. He couldn't go to the back or front without alerting Kiera's kidnapper. He assessed as he went. He looked for weak points—places that he could use to his advantage and get in unnoticed, unheard. The basement windows were the old pullout-with-a-lever kind. Easy to break into. He could squeeze into the basement in a pinch. It was a relief to focus on moving forward and not on what Kiera might be enduring now, at this moment.

Within seconds he was in. He dropped onto an empty concrete floor. He pressed his back against the concrete wall as he listened for noises. His heart pounded like it never had before as he feared that despite his reaction time, he might still be too late. The fear came from the fact that he could sense the emptiness. There was no life down here. He was alone. It was what he expected, and what he hoped not to find, not to be too late. He pulled out his pocket flashlight, shining it in a close range around him before spreading the beam out. There was nothing but one big concrete space. There was no development, no collection of stuff except for a trio of cardboard boxes. It was as if it was only temporary housing and not someone's home. There was shuffling upstairs, followed by a woman's cry.

He moved to the foot of the stairs. He wanted to run up and crash the party, but he couldn't. Waiting was going to kill him. He'd recognize that voice anywhere.

Kiera.

He held himself back. He couldn't burst onto the main floor. He had his gun at the ready, his breathing steady as he listened. He was trying to pinpoint the location of the sound. He heard a bang. Then, there was a sound like something or someone being dragged. He guessed they were not near the basement stairs, the sound seeming deeper, near the back of the house. He had nothing but guesses but he couldn't take the chance of wasting more time. He couldn't wait another second for every bit of time was working against Kiera. With his gun ready to fire on a second's notice he cautiously moved up the stairs. He felt with his feet in the dark, to avoid creaks that might warn of his presence. The basement door was closed. He put an ear to the door. There was silence on the other side. He couldn't pinpoint where Kiera's kidnapper was, where Kiera was—he had no visual. He had to take the chance.

He pushed the door quietly open. Nothing. He eased himself through the doorway, moving stealthily but quickly. He was at the junction of the kitchen and a hallway that led in two different directions. Left to a living area and right to what he guessed would be the bedrooms. He had his gun in both hands and the weapon led the way. He hung at the edge of the doorway. Time seemed to stand still and then he saw her. Just like that his eyes met Kiera's and his heart sank to see her bound and gagged, sitting on an old-style metal-legged kitchen chair. Before he could make a move in her direction, another movement had him turning to see a gun leveled at him. A middle-aged woman with an overtanned and wrinkled face glared at him but it was the gun in her hands that had his attention. He ducked and rolled away from Kiera, taking the trajectory of any bullet meant for him, away from her.

He came up on one knee in midroll. He was ready to shoot, to kill, to get Kiera the hell out of there. Her captor had retreated through the doorway that led to the living room. It wasn't a clean shot, but he took it anyway. She ducked behind the sofa. He moved forward and stopped.

A shot to his left took out a chunk of the doorframe. He ducked down as she jumped up and ran for the front door. He had a glimpse of her long black hair as she hunkered down. He didn't have a clear shot and took out his own chunk of drywall. Hunched and still moving, she turned and fired at him again. Plaster rained down on him; his vision blurred from the bits that got in his eye. He shot anyway, trying to take her out before she escaped or at best cause an injury. But she was out the door and gone.

He moved to the doorway; she was already in her van and taking off. He backtracked and checked the other two rooms of the house—empty.

"Kiera," he said, torn between chasing her kidnapper or making sure she was safe. There wasn't a choice. He needed to get Kiera out of here. Hopefully, his reinforcements had arrived. And they could take care of the woman who'd abducted her. She was the woman who might well be an accomplice to multiple murders. She'd meet her own judge and jury once the feds had her. In the meantime, the feds had his location both from his phone call to James and even without, they could easily track his phone. The latter he knew they would do despite his call, in case something changed. He put in a quick call to James to let him that Kiera's kidnapper had taken off in the white van he'd reported earlier. He didn't wait for much of a response before disconnecting.

He knelt down in front of Kiera. She looked at him with her heart in her eyes and fright in the trembling of her hands.

"It'll be okay—I'll get you out of here."

She nodded and there wasn't a trace of doubt in her demeanor.

Within seconds he had the rope untied, the cloth out of her mouth.

"Let's go," he said taking her arm. There was no time for explanation, no time for comfort. He needed her out of here and safe.

"My legs won't stop shaking," she said with a quiver in her voice.

His arm was around her waist as he helped her down a small flight of stairs and out the back door. He got her into the SUV. As he was walking around the vehicle he was on the phone, giving James more detail on what had occurred. He hung up after getting a promise that reinforcements were on the way. Seconds later, he shoved the phone in his pocket and was in the driver's seat backing the SUV out and away.

"Where are we going?" she asked.

"FBI headquarters here in Denver," he replied. "The man I report to, James, will meet us there."

She didn't say anything. He took her silence as acceptance or shock. He might need to get her medical attention. Although she didn't look like she'd been physically hurt.

"Are you okay?"

"Are you asking do I need a doctor?" she said in a soft voice that was unlike her. "If you are, I'm physically fine," she said with a hint of steel in her voice. "I don't need a doctor. I need this creep caught."

Silence fell between them, but he expected that. She'd been through hell and survived imminent death. He didn't expect her to say much, not now when she was still in shock.

He was only two blocks away from the house where she'd been held when he saw the white van. It was coming at them from the opposite direction. It was driving erratically, weaving and on the wrong side of the road.

"Hell," he muttered as he swung the vehicle around with a screech of tires. "Hang on," he said as he took a corner too sharp and headed away from the van and toward where he knew there was an unpopulated area. A crash from behind and the impact sent the SUV flying. He had to manhandle the steering wheel to keep the vehicle on course.

He cursed under his breath. And regretted it immediately as he glanced at Kiera. She didn't seem to notice. It was almost like she had checked out. Considering everything she had gone through, that made sense. The van hit them again. There was no way he needed this nut job trying to drive her van up his rear in an area like this. He swung left heading for a more industrialized area. There, where litter and empty lots quickly began to replace housing, there was no danger to others. It was a few blocks north. He'd seen it coming in and soon he was there, in a run-down and seemingly abandoned industrial area. Rusted machinery replaced houses. He put his foot on the gas. With the residential housing behind him, he turned the steering wheel as hard as he could, swinging the SUV completely around before bringing it to a sudden halt.

"Get down," he said to Kiera. "And no matter what happens, stay down."

She nodded. Her face was pale, her lips were set. But she looked more determined than frightened.

He was out of the SUV, his gun in hand as the white van screeched to a halt in front of them and the woman jumped out. This was the first time he'd gotten a close look at her. In the parking lot, it had been more distant. And her eyes had never met his. Now she met him head-on. There was evil in those eyes or maybe that was just fantasy. He was too far away to tell. He needed to focus on reality, on her and what he might need to do. After all, this was the woman who had threatened Kiera's life not once but twice—and if Kiera's story checked out, three times.

"I'm a US marshal. Drop your weapon," he ordered.

She kept walking toward him.

He had seconds to make the assessment. Seconds to take in the face of evil framed by long black hair streaked with gray. She looked like she'd been through hell and that had defined her face. He blew the thoughts off—this wasn't the time.

"Stop and drop your weapon or I'll shoot."

She hesitated and kept coming. The thought ran through his mind that she wanted him to kill her. Was it possible? Was she deliberately defying his order so that he could take her out? Whatever her reasons, she was giving him no choice with her weapon still aimed at him.

"Drop it!"

In the seconds that followed everything seemed eerily silent. She was still walking toward him. The distance between them quickly diminished from a hundred feet to fifty. He could give no more chances considering the fact that she hadn't even lowered her gun. He fired. And she fell. It seemed too simple, too easy. Just like that, it was over.

He heard a car door slam and next thing he knew Kiera was in his arms. He held her as if he would never let her go. And in his mind, he knew that if she agreed that's exactly what would happen.

Chapter Twenty-Five

Three days later

"If I could imagine hell, that would be it," James said
as they left the state prison.

Travis couldn't agree more. He knew that James
wasn't referring to the prison but to the life Eric had
been subjected to during his teenage years. Except
it was hard to feel any sympathy. For one, they both
agreed that what Eric had admitted was more of an attempt to shift blame and gain sympathy. If they didn't
know who Eric was and what he'd become, it might
have worked. As it was, the charming smile that he
offered them only added a creepy feel to the end of
a sordid tale. Eric was smart enough to end his tale
of woe at the point in the story where he was still the
victim. For they all knew that there was a point beyond that when the victim became the perpetrator. At
first, charming Eric would admit to none of that. He
stuck to his younger years, his own nightmare years.
There was no better word to describe the environment that had shaped Eric Solomon. What he'd done

to dozens of women was a different matter. When he spoke of the murders, it was always Susan's fault. He claimed that Susan had led the way. He wouldn't have done it, if Susan hadn't made him.

"That relationship was so twisted I don't think anyone could have made it up," James said. "It'll be one for the history books. A murderous woman prepping a teenage boy to be her partner for her future killing spree." He shook his head. "Unbelievable. Thank goodness these cases are rare. Hope we never have another."

"I'm with you on that," Travis said. "They both gave me the creeps."

In the end, despite a rough start, they'd gotten a full confession from Eric Solomon. On hearing that his partner, Susan Berker, was dead, his entire demeanor had changed. The tough-as-nails killer turned soft and frightened in seconds. In a way, he'd almost retreated to a juvenile phase. More important, he'd been willing to talk.

"He was her boy toy," Travis said referring to the killer behind bars and the now-dead woman. "And then he was so much more than that. I think given time, Eric could have become like her, maybe recruited his own team of killers."

"If she'd let him, that would mean stealing some of her power," James said practically. "In the end, he was every bit as guilty as she. They were in it together. What matters is he gave a full confession and neither of them will harm another woman again."

Travis nodded. It was a tragic, haunting story and

it was also an ugly story. It began with the tragedy and the teenage runaway, and it ended ugly when a woman took him in and taught him her own dark cravings. Susan had raised him from a teenager to a man and escalated their crimes as he matured. But she'd always led the show. She'd been who they should have been after from the beginning. But she'd fooled them all by putting Eric out in front, and literally brainwashing him to believe that he was leading the show. It had all been a lie. He'd been positioned, just in case she needed someone to take the fall.

THEY'D BEEN BACK in Cheyenne for a week. In that time Kiera hadn't been alone. Neither of them had wanted that. Travis wanted her with him, at his side. He wanted to wake up in the morning and know that she was there, safe. Most of all he wanted her, just flat out wanted her. So, he stayed at her condo.

It was late. But they'd been up watching a movie. He had a break between assignments and she hadn't returned to work yet. Without work the next morning, they'd lost track of time. He'd treated her with kid gloves since the rescue, holding her until she fell asleep, being by her side—watching out for her. It was all he could do to help her get over the nightmare.

"I'm going back to work next week. Don't try and convince me otherwise," she said abruptly.

"Actually, I was wondering what took you so long," he said with a serious edge to his voice.

"Really?"

"Let's say that I'm not surprised," he said with a

laugh. "And I'm not about to dissuade you. Just one ground rule, I'll drive you or you take a cab if I'm not available."

"Alright," she said.

He looked at her, surprised. That wasn't like Kiera. "What's up?"

"You'll see," she said with a laugh and rolled over and gave him a kiss that became a hot exploration before he pulled away.

"No," she said as she brought him back, her hand sliding down his belly and farther. He could feel himself get hard. He couldn't help it. Even a light touch, even a hint of what was to come had him hard and ready. Their clothes were gone in seconds. That's the way it always was—kid gloves didn't seem to make it to the bedroom. He put a hand over hers and with his other hand he began to run erotic patterns around her nipple, first one and then the other.

"Travis."

He silenced her with a kiss. They had all the time in the world and he was going to use that to his advantage. He ran his hand down, over her flat stomach, to the juncture of her thighs.

She inhaled sharply.

But her hands were soon working some magic of their own.

"Kiera," he began.

"I'm with you," she said hoarsely. "Let's do this."

He smiled. In another situation, he would have outright laughed. But that was Kiera's language of love. Or at least that was the way he thought of it. She had an odd way of expressing herself in the bedroom. He'd discovered that the first time he'd made love to her. And she'd repeated the odd phrase *let's do this* every time since. Now, he just considered it part of the norm. Life with Kiera would be challenging and passionate. Those thoughts disappeared as he focused on one thing and one woman.

"Travis," she said hoarsely. There was a pleading tone to her voice. He knew what she wanted. He knew what he wanted. They both wanted the same thing.

His other hand was still on her nipple as soon he had her body convulsing toward him. When he reached for a condom and entered her long minutes later it was only to the murmur of her voice and her promises of never-ending love. A man couldn't ask for more.

Epilogue

"I can't believe it's over," Kiera said.

Travis nodded. It had only been a week since Kiera had given her testimony and considering the atrocity of the crimes and their extent, the trial had gone quickly. While Eric Solomon had never repeated the admissions of guilt he'd revealed while awaiting trial, what they had was enough. He was now awaiting sentencing.

"Do you think it would have been different for Eric if he hadn't met Susan?" Kiera looked at him with a frown. "Was he flawed from the beginning, always meant to become a twisted killer?"

"I don't know. What I do know is that in the end, he was a grown man who had allowed himself to be molded into a sadistic killer. The boy was long gone," Travis said. The man would pay for what he had done, he thought.

In the last month, he'd insisted that Kiera take a

self-defense class. His work made him well aware that anything could happen. When she'd completed that she'd informed him that she was setting up a safe-ride program so that the workers in care homes through-out the city would be safe going home late at night or early in the morning. And she was thinking ahead, thinking that something might be set up through the city for other women who worked late or early hours and might not be able to afford a cab, but needed a worry-free ride home.

Some things had changed but some had stayed the same. Despite all her plans, Kiera still insisted that she had time to volunteer at the shelter. He'd been hesitant about that and as a result he found himself volunteering right beside her. He'd soon discovered that it wasn't dangerous, that the people there were disadvantaged, exactly as she'd told him. The saying she'd tossed at him had held true—you couldn't paint everyone with the same brush.

"What are you thinking about?" Travis asked. "About the trial?"

She looked up at him. "No," she said. "I'm done with that."

This time, he believed her. For they'd already talked about everything. They didn't need to talk about it again. It was over and eventually she'd be able to put the experience on a shelf labeled Night-mare. That's what it was, a nightmare that was over. A nightmare that would never happen again, not to her—and if he could help it, not to any other woman.

Travis's arm was over her shoulders and her skin

was soft against his lips as he kissed her neck and whispered in her ear. "What do you have planned for tonight?"

She looked up at him with the hint of the smile. "I heard a certain sexy marshal was going to cook me supper and woo me over dessert."

"Woo?" he said with a laugh. "Where did you dig that word up?"

A meow from the carrier had her smiling up at him. "Lucy was a hit," she said.

He smiled. This week she'd not just taken Lucy to the care home but she'd stopped at the local animal shelter and taken two other cats from there for their first visit. It was impossible to keep up with her. He'd never met a woman more motivated to help others, or a woman more able to do it.

"How'd it go?"

"There were half a dozen residents who love cats and each had had more than one in their lifetime. Lucy had more than her share of attention. And the other two cats turned out to be perfectly behaved. They'll definitely be back." She looked at him. "There's something else…"

His smile dropped. Something else he'd learned in the weeks that they'd dated, in the weeks since he'd asked her to marry him and since she'd said yes and made him happier than he'd ever been in his life—that when she said there was something else, he should run for cover.

The most recent time she'd said that phrase meant that she thought that Lucy needed company. Fortunately, she'd solved that by taking the cat to work more frequently. The time before that she'd thought that she should meet his family.

That had meant him spending an afternoon grilling and entertaining his folks and assorted relatives. Not that he didn't love seeing them, it was just that Kiera didn't believe in waiting on anything. He had forty-eight hours' notice. And it had been a pile of work—worth it in the end. Still, he cringed when she began with something that meant she had an idea, usually something she was passionate about. He'd learned that there was a lot she was passionate about. Some of it he appreciated, like how she kept their bed and their sex life imaginatively hot. Although, he admitted, it wasn't as if he didn't do his share. Their bedroom was on fire most nights.

He waited wondering what it was this time.

"I'd like to add to the guest list."

He nodded. That seemed fairly straightforward. He'd asked her to marry him in a traditional way—he'd gotten down on one knee, ring in hand. Now they'd agreed on a small wedding in the backyard of the condo they'd bought only a month ago. The wedding was in three weeks and invitations to the fifty invited guests had just gone out; another would be no problem at all.

"Ann, one of the seniors at the home, would like to come. We could get a disabled bus for them."

"Them?" he asked wondering when Ann had become plural.

"Well, if Ann wants to go, I know there'll be others. I thought it would only be fair to invite them all."

"Twenty," he said.

"And the workers."

He did the mental math. Forty people, as the numbers of staff when you factored shifts equaled the residents.

She smiled, as if sensing where his thoughts were going. "They won't all come."

"But most will," he said with a resigned smile. "And some are already invited," he said thinking of a couple of workers who were Kiera's friends.

"Possibly," she agreed. "But there are a few volunteers, as well."

"Whatever you want, sweetheart."

He wondered if the guest list was yet solid or if there'd be more. And he imagined there would be more surprises after the wedding. Her generous spirit was only part of what he loved about her. He leaned over and kissed her again, and this time the kiss was hot and passionate as he held nothing back.

"Forever and always," she said against his lips. "I love you, Travis Johnson."

"Back at you," he said. In his life he'd never thought he'd meet her. The woman who would love him passionately and unconditionally. He'd thanked the heavens on more than one occasion that her horrific experience hadn't changed her. She was the love of his life and now that he had found her, he knew that he'd never let her go.

He couldn't wait for the wedding. It was going

to be one hell of a day: family, friends, a busload of seniors and one very pampered cat. And, with three weeks to go, he never knew who or what might be added to the list. It wasn't going to be the beautiful, everything-is-coordinated kind of wedding. He imagined the wedding might well reflect the life to come. He couldn't see himself ever getting bored from that day forward.

"Always and forever," he whispered against her lips as he kissed her long and hard, sealing a pact that he knew could be nothing less than forever.

* * * * *

*Look for the next book in
Ryshia Kennie's American Armor miniseries,*
Marshal on a Mission,
available next month!

Get 4 FREE REWARDS!

We'll send you 2 FREE Books plus 2 FREE Mystery Gifts.

Harlequin Intrigue® books feature heroes and heroines that confront and survive danger while finding themselves irresistibly drawn to one another.

FREE Value Over $20

CHAPTER ONE

She struggled to surface from the black hole trying to suck
her back down. Her head hurt and she could barely open her
eyes. Every part of her body ached so badly she began to
think death would be a relief. But her heart, buried behind
bruised and broken ribs, beat strong, pushing blood through
her veins. And with the blood, the desire to live.

Willing her eyes to open, she blinked and gazed through
narrow slits at the dirty mud-and-stick wall in front of her.
Why couldn't she open her eyes more? She raised her hand
to her face and felt the puffy, blood-crusted skin around
her eyes and mouth. When she tried to move her lips, they
cracked and warm liquid oozed out on her chin.

Her fingernails were split, some ripped down to the quick,
and the backs of her knuckles looked like pounded hamburger

meat. Bruises, scratches and cuts covered her arms.

She felt along her torso, wincing when she touched a bruised rib. As she shifted her search lower, her hands shook and she held her breath, feeling for bruises, wondering if she'd been assaulted in other ways. When she felt no tenderness between her legs, she let go of the breath she'd held in a rush of relief.

She pushed into a sitting position and winced at the pain knifing through her head. Running her hand over her scalp, she felt a couple of goose egg–sized lumps. One behind her left ear, the other at the base of her skull.

A glance around the small cell-like room gave her little information about where she was. The floor was hard-packed dirt and smelled of urine and feces. She wore a torn shirt and the dark pants women wore beneath their burkas.

Voices outside the rough wooden door made her tense and her body cringe.

She wasn't sure why she was there, but those voices inspired an automatic response of drawing deep within, preparing for additional beatings and torture.

What she had done to deserve it, she couldn't remember. Everything about her life was a gaping, useless void.

The door jerked open. A man wearing the camouflage uniform of a Syrian fighter and a black hood covering his head and face stood in the doorway with a Russian AK-47 slung over his shoulder and a steel pipe in his hand.

Don't miss
Driving Force *by Elle James,*
available October 2019 wherever
Harlequin® books and ebooks are sold.

www.Harlequin.com

HIEXP0919

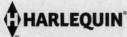

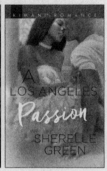

Love Harlequin romance?

DISCOVER.

Be the first to find out about promotions, news and exclusive content!

Facebook.com/HarlequinBooks

Twitter.com/HarlequinBooks

Instagram.com/HarlequinBooks

Pinterest.com/HarlequinBooks

ReaderService.com

EXPLORE.

Sign up for the Harlequin e-newsletter and download a free book from any series at **TryHarlequin.com.**

CONNECT.

Join our Harlequin community to share your thoughts and connect with other romance readers!
Facebook.com/groups/HarlequinConnection

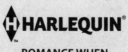

HARLEQUIN®

**ROMANCE WHEN
YOU NEED IT**

HSOCIAL2018

Earn points on your purchase of new Harlequin books from participating retailers.

Turn your points into **FREE BOOKS** of your choice!

Join for FREE today at
www.HarlequinMyRewards.com.

Harlequin My Rewards is a free program (no fees) without any commitments or obligations.

MYR18